The Girl Who Rode the Wind

Stacy Gregg

HarperCollins *Children's Books*

First published in hardback in Great Britain by
HarperCollins *Children's Books* in 2015
This edition published in 2016
HarperCollins *Children's Books* is a division of HarperCollins*Publishers* Ltd,
1 London Bridge Street
London SE1 9GF

HarperCollins*Publishers*
1st Floor, Watermarque Building, Ringsend Road
Dublin 4, Ireland

The HarperCollins Children's Books website address is
www.harpercollins.co.uk

For Stacy's blog, competitions, interviews and more, visit
www.stacygregg.co.uk

21

ISBN 978–0–00–812431–1

Printed and bound by
CPI Group (UK) Ltd, Croydon, CR0 4YY

MIX
Paper from
responsible sources
FSC**™**
www.fsc.org
FSC™ C007454

FSC™ is a non-profit international organisation established to promote
the responsible management of the world's forests. Products carrying the
FSC label are independently certified to assure consumers that they come
from forests that are managed to meet the social, economic and
ecological needs of present and future generations,
and other controlled sources.

Find out more about HarperCollins and the environment at
www.harpercollins.co.uk/green

For Hilda, the budding equestrienne.

May your future be full of excitement,

adventure and wonderful horses...

The Contrada of the Wolf

It was almost midnight when I turned down the steep cobbled streets into the Via di Vallerozzi. I walked alone except for my shadow, a black companion in the lamplight.

At the entrance to the Contrada of the Wolf I raised my eyes to the bell tower and felt the knot in my belly tighten. I stepped up to the door and knocked, rapping four times then four again. Then I waited, counting my heartbeats. I was about to try once more when I heard footsteps and then the creak of ancient hinges as the heavy oak door opened.

The guardsman, thin and sallow-skinned, shoulders hunched with age, poked his head out. He looked at me warily.

"Hello, signor…" My accent gave me away straight off. I didn't have the chance to say anything more.

"No tourists, Americano!" the guardsman grunted dismissively. "Not on the night before the Palio."

He began to close the door and I had to thrust my arm out to stop it shutting in my face.

"I'm not a tourist!" I insisted. "I'm Lola. Lola Campione."

I had expected my name to mean something to him, but there was no flicker of recognition on his stony face.

"Go find the Capitano. Tell him I'm here."

The guardsman didn't move. "The Capitano is in a meeting. Very important. He cannot be disturbed." He pushed the door and I felt it closing against me.

"No! Please don't –"

"Drago!"

From behind the guardsman a voice rang through the dark corridor.

"Come now, Drago," the voice said. "Do you not recognise this girl? This is the fantino herself. Let her in."

The guardsman hesitated, the look on his face made it plain that he was unimpressed. You're kidding me, right? *This twelve-year-old kid's the fantino?* Then, grudgingly, he did as he was told, releasing his grip on the door so that I could push it wide enough to move past him and come inside.

The hallway was lit by oil lamps that illuminated the dusty paintings on the wood-panelled walls. In this gloomy half-light a man with thick black hair, a sculpted beard and dark eyes stood in the centre of the room, dressed in floor-length black and white robes trimmed with brilliant orange.

"Hello, Capitano," I said.

"Good evening, Lola," he replied. "We were not expecting you tonight. Is something wrong?"

"I couldn't sleep," I said. "I was worried about Nico."

"I am touched by your concern," the Capitano said, not sounding touched at all. "I can assure you he is quite safe and well."

"I need to see him," I said. "I won't leave until I know he's OK."

"It is not possible, Lola," the Capitano replied.

"No one can see him tonight, not even you."

He grasped my arm and began to escort me back towards the front door. "You should go home. Get some sleep…"

I resisted, jerking my elbow away and pulling free of him. Standing at his post by the door the guardsman saw me do this and reached for his sword. The Capitano had to raise his hand to quell him.

"Lola, I have no time for this." The Capitano glanced anxiously over his shoulder into the darkness of the hallway. From a room at the far end, I could hear the muffled voices of men arguing in rapid-fire Italian.

"The rival contradas are here," he said. "We are discussing arrangements for the race tomorrow. I must ask you to leave."

The Capitano resumed his attempts to usher me to the door. I could see he was losing his patience, but I stood my ground.

"Let me see Nico. Please, Capitano? I've come all this way…"

When I said this, I only meant that it was a long distance to walk here, all the way from the villa, but the Capitano seemed to think my words had a deeper meaning.

"Yes, of course. It is a miracle, this journey you have made, Lola." He waved his hands dramatically. "From New York to Italy, you have come home to us, your people. And tomorrow you will ride in the greatest race in the world, the Palio, for the glory of the Lupa, the Contrada of the Wolf. Everything depends on you, Lola."

The conversation in the room beyond had become a shouting match. The Capitano was flustered, anxious to get back to his meeting.

"Very well, Lola," he said abruptly. "I will allow it. But it is against all the rules of the Contrada so you must tell no one. Are we agreed?"

I nodded.

"Then quickly, come with me."

I followed the Capitano down the hallway, through one of the many doorways that led off the main corridor.

The room we entered had a high vaulted ceiling and walls lined with antique glass cabinets. Behind the glass, headless mannequins were dressed in

Romeo and Juliet costumes with swords and flags, and suits of armour propped up behind them. It looked like a museum exhibition – except tomorrow all these glass cases would be opened up and the museum would come to life.

"Quickly, Lola!" The Capitano kept me moving past the display.

We continued through a labyrinth of secret rooms and passages that would have been impossible to navigate on my own. I stuck close as the Capitano took one turn after another, until we reached a narrow corridor that led to an iron door. On the door was the head of a wolf, cast in black iron, life-sized with two crossed swords behind it and eyes made from grey stone. Those eyes! They seemed to glare at me, challenging me. The wolf looked so lifelike, its muzzle jutting out, jaws open and teeth bared. If it had sprung from the door snarling and snapping I wouldn't have been at all surprised.

Beside me, the Capitano began muttering away, strange words that I didn't recognise, an incantation in Italian that seemed to be some kind of ancient ritual. As he spoke he raised his hands up, palms spread out in front of the wolf's head, then he placed both hands upon the hilts of the swords and pulled down hard. The swords acted as levers, splitting the wolf's face in two and opening the doors to reveal what lay on the other side, a spiral of stone stairs descending into darkness.

I waited, expecting the Capitano to go on ahead, but he stepped back away from the edge of the stairwell to make room for me to pass him.

"You must go alone from here. I need to return to my meeting."

And with that he turned and left me at the top of the stairs.

I peered down into the pitch-black, my heart hammering. I had to do this. Nico was down there and I hated to think of him alone and terrified in this strange place. I put out my hands, my fingertips brushing the cold stone wall to find my bearings, then I took my first step and began my descent into the darkness.

Feeling my way, shuffling along, I went down step by step until I reached the base of the stairwell. Here, I groped blindly until I clasped the cool iron of a door handle. Gripping it, I pushed as hard as I could and the door groaned open to reveal a narrow stone corridor lit by torches. I was underneath the rooms of the contrada. Ahead of me, I could see a door with a tiny window of heavy iron bars, like a prison cell.

"Hello?" My voice echoed down the corridor and I heard a snort in reply – the restless stamping of hooves on soft straw.

"Nico?"

It was him! He called back to me. Not his usual cheerful nicker, but a vigorous and frantic high-pitched whinny.

"Nico! It's OK!" I ran to the door and began to work the bolt. "I'm here… Uugghhh!"

The bolt was stuck. I strained at the rusted metal, trying to force it open but it wouldn't move. I could see Nico on the other side of the bars, fretting and pacing, back and forth, flicking his head anxiously. "I'm coming, Nico. It's OK."

With a rush, the bolt finally came loose and I had the door open and was running to his side, flinging my arms around his golden neck, burying my face

14

deep in the coarse strands of his flaxen mane.

"Of course I came," I whispered. "You didn't think I would leave you here alone, did you? I'll always come for you, Nico, no matter what."

It broke my heart the way he leant in to me, nuzzling in with his muzzle pressed against me, snorting and blowing, making these strange snuffly noises I had never heard before, like he was talking to me, saying, "You took so long! I was so lonely!"

"I'm sorry, I came as soon as I knew," I murmured. "It's going to be OK, I'm here now, I'm with you."

I knew that being trapped in this basement stall would terrify him. Nico had never been left alone like this before. He'd grown up in the fields at Signor Fratelli's farm with the other horses by his side. Even at night when he was brought in to his loose box in the stables, he'd had their whinnies and nickers right next door for company To be brought here and kept in solitary confinement in this tiny, cramped stone cell must have felt like cruel punishment, when in fact it was supposed to be a sacred honour; the final stage before his ascent to glory.

But glory is for gods, not for horses. Nico didn't

know that he was part of an ancient ritual or that the hopes and dreams of an entire contrada were riding on him tomorrow. As far as he was concerned, the only thing on his back when he stepped out onto that racetrack would be me. It was for me alone that he would gallop until his legs buckled and his heart burst. He had the heart of a champion, my horse, I had known it from the very first moment I saw him. I took one look into those deep brown liquid eyes of his and I knew that he was special, that he was the one.

"A horse that's going to win has a light in their eyes," my Nonna Loretta always says. "You look hard enough, Piccolina, and you'll see it. The good ones burn inside with the desire to prove themselves."

My nonna can look at a horse and tell you straight off before it sets foot on the track whether or not it's gonna win. When I was little, she'd take me to the Aqueduct on race days and we'd spend hours at the birdcage, me perched on her hip, choosing winners as the horses paraded by.

"Can you see which one it will be, Piccolina?" she would ask. That's her nickname for me, Piccolina, it means *little one.*

I always chose the hot ones, of course. Won over by their flashy looks, I'd single out the horses that fretted and danced like prizefighters. They looked like they wanted to go fast.

"No, no, Piccolina!" Nonna would shake her head in disapproval. "You must look beyond the shiny coat and the pretty face. You need to look deeper, look at the heart."

"That's silly! I can't see their hearts, Nonna!" I would giggle.

"Try again," Nonna would say. And then she would give me a hint. "Look at that one over there. You see the way his ears pricked at the roar of the crowd in the grandstand? The flick of his tail when the jockey mounted? He has heart, Piccolina. I think he is the one."

"Should we bet on him then, Nonna?" I would ask.

"Oh no!" Nonna would say. "Racing is the sport of kings, but gambling is for fools and scoundrels. A Campione never bets."

That's our name, Campione. It means *Champion*

in Italian. Our stables are called Champion Racing. Not that the horses we train are champions. Often, by the time they come to us they are ten-time losers, and it's our job to turn them around because no one else will take them.

My dad, Ray Campione, was a pretty famous jockey back in the day, but he was always falling off and breaking bones, and after my mom died Nonna said it was too dangerous. She said if he fell again then us four kids could wind up being orphans, so Dad gave up riding and started training. He's supposed to be the head trainer, but everyone knows it's really Nonna who calls the shots, deciding the feed and workout regimes, which jockey will get the ride and when the horse is ready to run.

Nonna used to ride track, but she's too old for it now. "Eighty-five, Lola! How did that happen? I still feel sixteen." That's how old she was when she came to New York on her own, all the way from Italy. It was 1945. The war had just ended and she arrived on a boat at Ellis Island "with nothing except the clothes on my back and my jodhpurs and riding boots in a duffel bag".

Nonna never liked to talk about "the old country". I would try and ask her about what life was like back in Italy, but she never did say much. The only thing she would ever talk about was the horses. "They were Anglo-Arabs," she told me. "Very intelligent, beautiful creatures, quite different from these hot-heads we have to train!"

I didn't realise what she meant until I met Nico. He isn't like any horse I ever met in New York, or even any of the other horses he shares a stable with at the Castle of the Four Towers in Siena. He's enormous for a start, and he's showy with his rich honey-chestnut coat, white blaze and thick flaxen mane. He could almost be too pretty, except he's burly too; real powerful with these strong shoulders and haunches. If he wanted to, he could lash out with a hoof and kill you with a single blow, but he would never do that. He's sweet-natured and gentle as a faun. When I'm in the loose box with him I never even need to use a halter to restrain him. I can leave the doors wide open and he'll just stay in the stall with me like he wants to be here, shoving his muzzle up against me as I pet him, just like he's doing right now.

"Tomorrow," I tell him, "we're going to go out there and win this crazy bareback race in front of all of Italy, and when we cross the finish line we will be heroes and the contrada will remember us for ever."

The Palio is the world's most dangerous race. The horses are ridden by hard-bitten jockeys – men who won't think twice about using whatever means necessary to beat us if we get in their way.

"There are no saddles," I remind Nico. "And no rules either. The other horses will crash into you and their jockeys will whip and push me if they can get close enough."

Nico shakes his mane anxiously.

"Hey, hey, no…" I reassure him. "Don't worry, Nico. Those guys, they think they're tough, right? But they never met a girl from Ozone Park before."

It's not like I'm lying to him. Nico is my best friend and I would never do that. But he needs his jockey to be strong right now. If he realised the fantino was nothing more than a scared twelve-year-old girl then we'd both be in real trouble.

Lucky for me, if there's one thing I'm good at it is

acting tough when I am actually terrified. I guess I have Jake Mayo to thank for that.

It's funny to think that you owe a debt to the boy who made your life at middle school into a living hell, but in a weird way I wouldn't be here if it wasn't for Jake. Growing up in Ozone Park, I was already pretty battle-hardened before he started his own personal war against me. But after our fight, something changed deep inside of me. So if you want to know how I got here, then I'll tell you. It all started the day that I broke Jake Mayo's nose.

Fight

The linoleum in the hallway was pale blue with dark swirls. I stared down and imagined it was the sea, about to swell up beneath me and swallow me. As if I was that lucky.

"Miss Campione?" The door beside me opened and a bony finger curled out to beckon me in. I stood up and walked over the ocean and into Mr Azzaretti's office.

"I don't usually see you in here, Miss Campione." Mr Azzaretti moved around to his side of the desk and motioned for me to sit.

"No, sir."

"Do you want to tell me what happened?"

I shrugged my shoulders. "He was asking for it."

"Is that all you have to say?" Mr Azzaretti looked serious. "Because I've got a boy in sick bay right now with a broken nose and he's saying you did it."

A broken nose. I felt the blood rush to my cheeks. I broke Jake Mayo's nose?

Serves him right. I thought, but I didn't say it. I knitted my fingers together to stop my hands shaking. I was still charged full of adrenaline and my throat hurt from where Jake had held me. He was much stronger than me, a real all-American quarterback in the making. I'd only managed to throw that one punch before he'd lunged at me, locked his arm around my neck and dragged me to the ground. That was how the teachers had found us, squirming around on the asphalt, red-faced and sweaty with a circle of kids all around us chanting "Fight! Fight! Fight!"

Mr Azzaretti waited for me to say something while I looked down at my hands. There was a long silence between us and then he gave a sigh and pushed his chair away and stood up. He came right around and perched on the edge of the desk beside me. He was a tall, angular man. He always wore a shirt and tie, but he kept his sleeves rolled up as if he had proper manual work to do, like a groom at the stables instead of a middle-school principal.

"Lola." He said my name, and my heart sank. It was the softness of the word, the kindness in his voice, that made me realise I was in real trouble. "Do you know how much it concerns me to see the smartest kid in this school, a student I consider to be scholarship material, being called in because of this sort of behaviour?"

I could feel my eyes getting teary. "I'm sorry, Mr Azzaretti." I wiped them with my sleeve, noticing the bloodstain as I did so. That blood wasn't mine.

"You know I'm going to have to call this boy's parents?" Mr Azzaretti said. "And your dad too, obviously?"

I felt a flush of pleasure at the idea of Jake Mayo having to explain to his dad that a girl had broken his nose. It almost made it all worth it.

"My dad's asleep. He turns his phone off in the afternoons."

"All right," Mr Azzaretti said. "Then you'll give him this as soon as you get home and ask him to call

24

me, OK?" He handed me an envelope. "Tell him you've been suspended from school until further notice."

It was fourth period and everyone else was in math. I cut around the back of the science block and across the playground at the back of the school. I squeezed through the gap in the mesh fence and out onto Sutter Avenue. Usually I turned left here, towards Rockaway, but I could feel the weight of that note from Mr Azzaretti in my backpack. So I headed right instead, following the green mesh fence line behind the houses, making my way towards the Aqueduct grandstands.

My problems with Jake Mayo had started at the beginning of the term. Before then, I don't think he even knew my name. He hung out with the populars – Tori and Jessa and Ty and Leona - and I hung out with no one. Weird Lola Campione, the brainiac girl always with her nose in a book. Because if you have no one to hang out with in middle school then you need a book to read, because it stops you looking so lonely. I sound like I feel sorry for myself, but I don't really. I don't know why but I don't make friends easy. I'm shy, I guess, and I never know what to talk about with other kids because my life is all about horses.

Our family, we're "Backstretchers". That's what they call us on account of the fact that we spend our whole lives at the racetrack in the backstretch, the underground neighbourhood behind the grandstands at Aqueduct.

There are some backstretchers who actually live right there at the track twenty-four seven. They sleep in hammocks slung up in the loose boxes and eat all their meals in the bodega.

We don't live far from the track, just on the other side of Rockaway Boulevard in Ozone Park. Our house has four bedrooms, one each for Dad and Nonna and another for my two brothers, Johnny and Vincent. I share the downstairs bedroom with my big sister, Donna. She's nineteen and a total pain in the neck. She's got Dad wrapped around her little finger, so he treats her like a princess even though she is the only one who does nothing to help out with the family business. Johnny and Vincent both dropped out of school the day they turned sixteen to ride trackwork. So I only have four years to go. Except Dad won't let me quit school.

"Sweetheart," he says. "A clever girl like you, you could be a doctor or a lawyer or anything you want. You're going to stay in school and get a scholarship and go to college, Lola. There ain't no way you're gonna wind up like me."

Except I wasn't going to get a scholarship now, was I? Even Donna, who was always in trouble, had never actually been suspended. I didn't know how I was going to explain this to my dad. He was gonna hit the roof.

That morning I'd gone to Aqueduct as usual. I earn pocket money cleaning out the stalls. I stayed longer than I should have done because Fernando was settling in a new horse so I had to do his mucking out too. I was going to go home and get dressed for school, but I had no time, so I just changed my T-shirt, which was sweaty, and kept the same jeans and boots. I figured that was OK. The boots were my riding boots, scuffed brown leather, which I wore every day at the track. I gave them a wipe on the straw before I left the loose box to clean them off a bit and then ran the whole way to school.

By the time I got to the gates I was sweaty again and the bell had already rung. I like to arrive at class early because I have this favourite desk in the front row, but on this day all the desks up front were filled and the only spare seat left was near the back next to Jake Mayo.

I would have done anything to find another seat. Jake was in all my classes, but we'd never spoken, not once. Due to my terminal uncoolness I guess.

I excused my lateness to Miss Gilmore, flung myself down into my seat and opened my textbook as she began writing up stuff on the white board.

Jake was looking at me funny.

"Hey!" he hissed.

I ignored him.

"Hey, Campione!"

I looked up. "Yeah?"

"Where's your horse?"

There was laughter from Tori and Jessa who sat in the row behind us.

"Hey, Campione!" Jake leaned over towards me. "You know you smell of manure, right?"

I looked down at my boots. They were dirty from the stables I guess, but I hadn't really noticed. I would have changed them if I had time. Anyway, there was nothing I could do about it now. I pretended I hadn't heard him and began furiously copying down the lesson from the board.

Then suddenly, in front of everyone, Jake flung himself across his desk and began convulsing, coughing and spluttering like he was going to die or something. The whole class was watching him and Miss Gilmore stopped writing on the board.

"Are you all right, Jake?" she asked, looking concerned.

Jake stopped performing and sat up.

"Sorry, miss," he smirked. "It's like I can hardly breathe in here because of Campione! She stinks of horse poo!"

The whole class fell apart laughing at this and Jake gave me a look of satisfaction. His humiliation of me was complete.

I thought it would end there, but it didn't. At lunch he gave a whinny as he walked by me in the cafeteria and made a big deal of holding his nose. I could see him at his table with the other populars, all of them looking over and laughing about it.

I walked home that day and for the first time ever I couldn't wait to get out of my riding boots.

I didn't want to talk about it, but Nonna has a way of winkling things out of you. She could tell something was wrong and that night after dinner she sat down on my bed and we had a big talk.

"He'll have forgotten you by tomorrow, you'll see," my nonna said. "With a bully, you have to ignore them, like you don't care. Then this boy will give up and start on someone else."

"I am!" I insisted.

I kept on ignoring him, just like Nonna told me. But it didn't stop. The next day Jake managed to get the seat next to me again and spent the whole class whinnying at me, doing it under his breath, just quiet enough so the teacher couldn't catch him. He did the same thing in the playground every time he walked past me, and by the end of the week all the other kids were doing it too.

"Do you want me to talk to one of your teachers about it?" Nonna offered.

"No!" I was horrified. "No, honest, I'm fine. Just forget about it…"

I stopped talking about Jake at home. I was worried that Nonna would tell Dad and then the next thing I knew he'd be marching into school to "sort him out". I was desperate to avoid this happening – almost as desperate as I was for Jake to stop picking on me.

Dad worried about me in a way he'd never done with Johnny and Vincent, or even Donna. She had been a popular when she was at school. Now she was studying to be a beauty therapist, which accounted for the fact that she spent all her time at home practising her make-up in the mirror and painting her nails. We shared a closet – half each. Her half was overflowing. My half was all T-shirts and jeans.

"Can I try on one of your skirts?" I asked Donna.

"Why?" she looked suspicious.

"Because."

"As long as you don't ruin it."

I pulled out her blue skirt with the black spots.

"Can I wear this to school?" I asked.

"Since when do you wear skirts?" Donna arched her over-pencilled brow at me.

"Please, Donna?" I went red in the face.

"OK," she sighed. "I don't like that one anyway – you can have it."

I tried it on.

"It feels strange to have bare legs," I said.

"You have lovely legs," Nonna said.

"She has legs like hairy toothpicks!" Donna shot back.

"Donna, be nice to your sister!" Nonna Loretta warned.

"You need some shoes to wear with it," Donna pointed out.

I looked at myself in the mirror.

"All the populars wear white trainers," I said.

"Trainers?" Nonna asked.

"Yeah," I said. "Like white sports shoes."

I looked at the shoes in my half of the closet.

"I can wear these I suppose." I fished out my usual shoes – a pair of battered old red Converse and put them beside the skirt in my half of the closet.

The next morning, when I got home from helping Dad at the track, Nonna Loretta was waiting for me. She'd made me lunch and there was a box beside it on the kitchen table.

"What's in the box?" I asked.

"Take a look," she said.

They were white tennis shoes.

"I got them in a sports store on special," Nonna told me. "That's what they wear at school, yes?"

"They're not the same," I said. "These are tennis shoes."

Nonna didn't see the difference. "Try them on."

They fitted me.

"There! They look very nice," Nonna said.

On Monday I wore my new outfit to school. The skirt was a bit big so I put a belt on it. The shoes were so white they positively glared in the sunlight. I had English first period. I made sure I was early and got my usual seat at the front, but on the way out of class Jake caught up with me.

"Hey, Lola. Cool shoes."

I felt sick. He was being totally sarcastic.

How could I have been so dumb? The shoes were totally wrong! I wished I could have just taken them off and walked around in bare feet, but that wasn't allowed at school.

At lunchtime, I decided the best thing to do was go to the library so that no one would see my dumb white shoes. I was on my way across the playground when Jake spotted me. He was with Ty and Tori and Jessa. They began to walk towards me. There should have been a teacher on duty, but I couldn't see one.

"Hey, Campione!" Jake cocked his head so that his hair flopped to one side then he pushed it back coolly with his right hand. It was his trademark gesture, like he thought he was in a boy band. He was so vain about that hair; you could tell he spent hours on it each morning before school. It was shaved short up the back and the fringe was long so that it grazed perfectly against his tanned cheekbones.

"Where'd you get your shoes?"

I kept my eyes down. I tried to keep walking past him, but he stepped in front of me and blocked my way.

I stepped to the left and Jake did too. Then to the right, and he matched me, like we were dancing. I could feel my face burning with embarrassment.

Jake stepped in real close to me and then he gave an exaggerated sniff, wrinkling up his nose.

"You might want to change those shoes again, Campione." He grinned. "Because you still stink of horse poo!"

I heard the laughter buzzing in my ears and saw the smug look on Jake's face. And that was when I threw the punch that broke his stupid nose.

Dad broke eleven bones in his racing career. You could see how his collarbone stuck out funny from the time when a horse went up on its hind legs in the starting gate and crushed him against the barrier. Another time he spent a week in intensive care after a three-year-old he was breezing spooked at a car horn. Dad fell and another horse running behind him struck him with a hoof on the head, shattering his helmet into pieces and knocking him out cold.

He fit right in with the other jockeys in the bodega, sitting around shirtless, comparing battle scars as they drank endless cups of black coffee. Most of them were on crazy diets to keep thin enough to make racing weight. Dad liked to "mess with their heads" by sitting right beside them at the communal dining table and ordering a big breakfast from Sherry who ran the kitchen – sausages, beans, eggs and fried bread. You should have seen the half-starved look on the jockeys' faces as Dad sat there and ate his way through it all, groaning with pleasure and savouring every bite. He thought it was hilarious.

"I punished my body harder than any of them back in the day," Dad would say. "Taking saunas for hours before a race to sweat out the water weight and drinking those disgusting diet shakes." He would shake his head in disbelief. "Sometimes when I sat on a horse I was so weak from hunger I couldn't even hold him back. No wonder I fell so many times."

When I was little, instead of bedtime stories, I would get Dad to recount the tales behind all of his broken bones. He made a real drama out of it, acting out the whole race for me. He could recall every name of every single horse and its jockey, all the details of how he rode the race and where he was in the field at the moment he fell.

The best story by far was the one about the missing fourth finger on his left hand.

"The horse was called Forget-me-not," Dad would begin. "And when I got given the ride on him,

Lola, I was punching the air with the thrill of it! He was this big, black stallion, pure muscle and power, and he was the flat-out favourite in the Belmont Stakes. My cut of the purse would come to enough money to buy my own stables."

He would be telling me this as he sat on the side of my bed and I would be propped up on my pillows beside him in my pyjamas, wide-eyed, waiting for the rest of it as if I had never heard it before, even though I'd been told the story a thousand times.

"Anyway," Dad would continue, "the week before the race I'm breezing Forget-me-not, working him alongside a couple of other horses to get his blood up, when he gets crowded on the rail and panics, and I don't know what gets into his head, but all of a sudden he tries to jump the barrier! He breaks the whole railing and I must have been knocked out cold, because the next thing I know they're wheeling me into the hospital and I can feel this real sharp pain in my left hand. So they take me straight up to x-ray and the doctors take a look and it turns out my finger is broken in three places. Must have hit the rail as I went down."

I look at the missing place where Dad's finger used to be.

"So they cut it off?"

Dad shakes his head. "Not straight away. They tried strapping it up with tape, and said it just needed time to heal. But I had the Belmont the next week and that tape was no good. Even with a glove over the top I couldn't close the finger and grip the reins without screaming in pain. So I went back, told the doctors I needed painkillers, but the drugs they gave me, all they did was make me woozy. So I went back to them again, and do you know what I said?"

I did know, because I had heard this story before. And not just from Dad. I'd heard it from the other jockeys in the bodega. In the version my dad told me, he walked into hospital and insisted they remove his finger so he could ride.

But the way the other jockeys told it was even more gruesome. They said the surgeons refused to amputate and so my dad went back to the stables and got a wood block and a splitter axe and cut the finger off himself. Then, with his hand wrapped in a gamgee horse bandage, he caught a cab back to Jamaica Hills, showed the doctors the bloodied stump and told them to go ahead and stitch it up.

Dad rode in the Belmont Stakes that weekend minus his finger. Forget-me-not came in dead last.

I'm telling you this because you need to know the sort of man my dad is. So now you'll understand why I couldn't bring myself to go home and admit to him I'd been suspended from school.

Fernando was sweeping out the aisle between the loose boxes when I reached the stables.

"Lola!" he gave me a friendly wave. "You lookin' for Ray? He's long gone."

Dad finished working the last of the horses by midday. He'd have been up since four a.m. and he'd be home having his afternoon nap by now, just like I'd told Mr Azzaretti.

"I came to see the horses," I said.

Fernando looked at his watch. "No school today?"

"I finished early." This wasn't exactly a lie. "Can I help muck out the stalls?"

Fernando leant against his broom. "Maybe you can take out Ginger? I was gonna put him in the walker. You can do it while I finish up here?"

"Sure," I said.

In the tack room I threw down my backpack on a chair and gave it a sideways glance, thinking about that note, shoved down deep against my textbooks. Then I went over to the wall where all the halters were lined up and grabbed one.

Ginger had his head out over the door of the stall, waiting for me.

"Hey, Ginge." I gave him an affectionate scratch on his muzzle, but he flinched away from me. He wasn't very friendly. Most of the horses in Dad's stables were grumpy, to tell the truth. Ginge was the worst of them all – he was a biter. Last week he had bitten Tony the groom's finger when he went to slip on his halter, pretty much taking the skin clean off with his teeth. Dad said Tony had screamed like a girl – which I found insulting because I don't scream.

Anyway, Tony should have known better because everyone knew you had to watch Ginge like a hawk when you were tacking him up. All I needed to do today to put him on the walker was put his halter on and lead him across the yard. The walker was this big circular machine – the horses went inside the cage and you turned the engine on and the walker kind of scooched them along from behind, so they had to keep going in circles, a bit like a playground roundabout, turning them round and round. It gave them exercise on days when there was no jockey to ride them.

I was about to slip the halter on when I had a much better idea.

"Fernando?"

I stuck my head around the corner of the loose box. "I'm gonna jog Ginge, OK?"

Fernando stopped digging at the straw. "You what? Since when are you riding track, Lola?"

"It's OK," I told him. "Dad said I could do workouts – not on Sonic and Snickers, but just with the horses that aren't the big shots, like Ginge and Cally."

I liked this lie. It sounded believable that Dad would let me ride the horses that were pretty much already failing as three-year-olds. The other day I'd heard him say that Tiger, our moggie cat, had more chance of winning the Preakness than Ginger did.

Fernando shrugged. "Easier to put him in the walker, but if you want to ride, kid, and your dad's OK with it, you go right ahead."

Ginge had his ears back the whole time as I tacked him up, looking real moody about it, as if he'd been having a nice quiet time before I interrupted his day. But once we were actually out from the stalls and on the track, he obviously felt differently. His ears pricked forward and with each stride he gave a quick, enthusiastic snort like he was humming a tune to himself.

I made him walk at first, until he got used to the sights and sounds. There was a ride-on mower trimming the infield, and he spooked a little as it went past so I had to reassure him. Ginge usually raced in blinkers because he was prone to spooking and being distracted. I let him have a good hard look at that ride-on and then I clucked him up to a trot.

Racehorses are like athletes. They have a workout programme devised just for them. One day they'll be jogging, just trotting along to loosen up their muscles. The next day they'll be breezing – going almost flat out at a gallop, but still not quite at racing speed.

I'd told Fernando I was gonna jog, but by the time I reached the back straight, I decided it wouldn't do any harm to try Ginge at a gallop.

I rocked up high in the saddle and put my legs on, asking him to go faster, and the trot became a canter. Ginge was snorting and huffing beneath me, and when I urged him on some more he reluctantly picked up the pace into a slow, loping gallop. That was Ginge all right. He'd never won a race and it drove Dad mad because he knew Ginge had speed in him. He was just stubborn about showing it.

"Come on, Ginge," I coaxed him. "Let me see what you've got."

Nothing. I was hustling him along, kicking and pumping my arms, but Ginge refused to go any faster.

We rode almost three furlongs like that and then, as we swept around the far side of the track, I heard this almighty crack. The ride-on mower had backfired. It sounded just like a gunshot and it put a shock through Ginge like a lightning bolt. He spooked violently and I felt him suddenly skitter out sideways from underneath me. For a sickening moment I thought I was gonna fall, but somehow I managed to stay with him and get my balance back. He was so strong against my hands, stretching out flat at a gallop. I don't know what made me do it, but instead of trying to pull him back, I let him run. "Go on, then! Go!"

Ginge's hooves pounded out like thunder against the soft loam, as I perched up there on his back, urging him to go faster and then a little more again until we were flying.

The wind was so strong in my face it stung my eyes. I had tears streaming down my cheeks, and even though they weren't real ones, it felt so good to cry. I was racing the wind and everything that had happened that day got left behind in my wake and I was myself again and I was free.

Back around by the exit to the stables I pulled Ginge up at last and brought him back to a jog. He was blowing so hard that I had to do another whole lap of the track at a walk to cool him down, and then I leapt down and led him back to the stables.

"That didn't look like no jog to me." Fernando glared at me as I brought Ginge through to his stall. "This horse has to race on the weekend, you better not be messing with his training."

I shook my head. "Sorry, Fernando, I tried to pull him up, but he took off on me and I couldn't hold him."

Fernando looked at me with an air of resignation. "You think I'm a fool, Lola? I know what you were doin' out there."

He took Ginger's reins and I thought he was in a bad mood with me until he cast a look back over his shoulder and smiled. "You ride track real good. You look just like Ray out there."

Just like my dad.

That was all I ever wanted to be.

The Bet

My brother Johnny glared at the spaghetti on his plate. "C'mon. Are you kidding me?"

"What's your problem now?" Dad asked.

Johnny poked at it with his fork. "Is that all I get? Where's the rest of it?"

"It's enough." My dad ignored his complaint and carried on dishing up meatballs to the rest of us. "You know the deal. You want to ride track, you gotta watch your diet."

"I do!" Johnny insisted.

"Sure," my dad grunted. "So that must be why I saw you at Dunkin' Donuts on the way home after workouts this morning."

Vincent gave a hoot of delight. "Busted!"

"Yeah, laugh it up, brother!" Johnny jabbed his fork at him.

I kept cutting into my meatball.

"You're very quiet this evening, Lola," Dad said.

"I'm hungry, that's all," I said.

I was hoping he wouldn't ask me about school because if he asked me straight up then I would have to confess that I had been suspended. That note from Mr Azzaretti was still there, glowing out at me like neon from my school bag in the corner of the room.

My dad cast a glance at Nonna, as if she might have an insight as to why I was so silent, but she gave a shrug as if to say she had no idea and so Dad let it drop.

"Loretta." He cleared his throat. "You remember that Ace of Diamonds filly that Frankie was training last season?"

Nonna nodded. "You mean the bay with the white socks on the hind legs?"

"That's her," my dad said. "Well, you always said you thought she had star quality. Frankie thought so too. He sent her off to Lance Barton's stables in

Kentucky and the word is she's been breaking three-year-old records on the training track there in every single workout."

"Is she ready to race?" Nonna asked.

My dad nodded. "This Thursday at Churchill Downs is her maiden. Frankie's told me on the down-low that she's a sure bet to win it. And the odds, Loretta." My dad's voice dropped to a low whisper. "She's paying out at seventy-three to one."

Nonna Loretta's face fell.

"Absolutely not, Raymond!"

"Listen –" my dad began, but he was cut dead by Nonna.

"No, Ray, you listen to me! How many rules do we have in this family?"

There was silence around the table. None of us dared to speak when Nonna was in full flight like this.

"Two rules, Ray!" Nonna sure had a powerful voice for a little old lady. "Two rules that the Campiones live by. We don't bet on horses and we don't tell lies."

I felt myself curl up a little, trying to make myself

48

smaller as she said this.

"But, Loretta!" My dad bounced back. "This horse, she's a machine. She's gonna win by ten lengths and nobody will ever see it coming! And seventy-three to one! Maybe even more. The bookies will –"

"The bookies will take your money because that's what bookies do," Nonna Loretta said stonily.

My dad took a deep breath. "I'm telling you…"

"No, Ray," Nonna said. "I'm telling you. The racing business is how we make our money, but betting on races is different. That's a sure-fire way of losing the lot. We've made it this far without betting on horses, haven't we?"

My dad sighed. "All right, all right. I thought, just this once…"

Nonna's scowl deepened.

"OK," Dad said. "I get it. No betting, period. OK?"

"Aww, c'mon," Donna groaned. "Can't he place just a little bet, Nonna? There are these new high heels that are on sale right now at Macy's that I would love…"

Donna saw the look on Nonna Loretta's face and

shut her mouth real quick.

I didn't say a word. I was just glad that the whole argument had taken the attention away from me and while they'd all been talking, I'd been busy cleaning my plate.

"May I be excused, please?" I asked.

"You've finished already?" Nonna raised an eyebrow.

"Sure, Lola," Dad said. "Have you got homework tonight?"

"No," I said truthfully. "No, I don't."

As I left the table I heard Nonna Loretta ask my dad, "So that filly Frankie tipped you off on. What's her racing name?"

"Aces High," my dad replied.

It was a good name, I thought. I don't know much about playing poker but I'm pretty sure that aces high usually wins.

The next morning I said goodbye to Nonna and started walking to school. I took the usual cut-through at Sutter Street, clambering through the fence into the park. And that was where I stopped.

I sat there on the swing set, rocking back and forth and thinking about what to do.

I had never told a lie like this before. The problem was, I had left it too long now to come clean and had made it worse. I got down off the swings and sat inside the playground's plastic crawly tunnel for a bit, worried that I would get seen by someone if I stayed out in the open for too long. Then I realised I was acting ridiculous. I couldn't turn up here every day and hide in a plastic tube. I had to tell the truth. I had to go and talk to Dad.

It was almost ten o'clock by the time I reached the track. Dad would have finished working the last of the horses by now. He would be back in his office doing the paperwork.

Dad called it an office, but really it was just a loose box like the ones the horses used, except with a desk and a filing cabinet in it, instead of straw on the floor.

I was walking past the stalls when I heard the sound of hoof beats behind me.

"Hey, Lola!"

It was Johnny and Vincent. They had just finished

a workout; both their horses were sweating and blowing.

"I've got to see Dad," I said, ignoring them and walking towards the office.

"I wouldn't go in if I were you," Vincent said.

I kept walking.

"Mr Azzaretti is in there."

I turned around. "Are you serious?"

"What's going on, Lola?" Johnny asked. "It must be pretty bad if old man Azzaretti is making house calls."

Johnny and Vincent were always in trouble at school, but never once had they been in enough trouble for Mr Azzaretti to turn up at our place. That achievement was mine alone.

"Maybe you should go home, Lola?" Johnny looked worried. "We'll tell Dad you were —"

As he said this, the door to the office opened and Dad walked out, with Mr Azzaretti beside him.

Mr Azzaretti looked relieved to see me. "Well, at least we don't have to file a missing persons report," he said.

Dad, on the other hand, looked furious. "Do you

know the trouble you've put Mr Azzaretti to? He came all this way down to see me, taking time out of his day because he wanted to know how you were doing and why I hadn't contacted the school about your suspension. So I say 'What suspension? My Lola's at school right now' –"

"Dad," I broke in. "I'm sorry. I know I should have said something sooner, but I was coming to tell you now."

"Anyway," Mr Azzaretti said. "I don't see any reason to involve the school further now that you've turned up. It's family business as far as I'm concerned." He turned to my dad. "I'll leave this with you, Ray."

My dad shook his hand. "Thanks, Arlo, you know how much I appreciate you coming by."

"She's a good kid, Ray," Mr Azzaretti said, as if I wasn't standing right there. "The brightest in her year. I hate to see her mess it up, that's all."

He gave me a very stern look as he said this, and then he turned and walked away. No one said anything and the only sound was Mr Azzaretti's shoes in the corridor until he was gone.

"Get in the car, Lola," my dad said. "We're going home."

I was prepared for Dad to tear strips off me. What I wasn't able to handle was the silent treatment. All the way home he said nothing. It wasn't until we were getting out of the car that he spoke to me.

"Why did you do it, Lola?"

"Because he was bullying me," I said, tears welling up in my eyes. I hated crying. I never cried. "He was teasing me and he wouldn't stop, no matter what, and then he started going on about my shoes and they were the ones that Nonna bought me and I just couldn't stand it any more and I hit him."

"You should have told me about it," my dad said. "You know how lucky we are that his parents aren't pressing charges?"

"I'm sorry." I was sobbing now. I thought he was gonna be furious, but he just put his arm around me and gave me a hug.

"My girl can throw some punch, huh?" He ruffled my hair. "That Mayo kid won't mess with you again, I bet."

When Johnny and Vincent found out, they both

thought it was hilarious. At dinner, they started calling me "slugger". Like "Hey, slugger, can you pass the salt?" "Hey, slugger, want some mashed potato?"

"Enough! This is not a laughing matter," Dad warned them.

"Why aren't you punishing her?" Donna said, glaring at me. "She's always getting away with stuff."

"I got suspended!" I shot back at her.

Nonna gave me a pat on the hand. "Lola was only defending herself," she said. "You take on a Campione and that's what you get. That boy is lucky I don't go around to his house and break his nose for him again!"

I was suspended for the rest of term, which was another three weeks and then it was Summer Vacation – almost three months without school! Dad had tried to talk Mr Azzaretti into letting me back sooner, and he would have allowed it, but he said the school board made the rules and there was no way around it. I would have to stay home and be sent homework assignments and class work so that I didn't slip behind.

"If I do my school work in the afternoons can I come to the track with you in the mornings?" I asked Dad. "I can help Fernando and I could even work some of the horses."

Dad shook his head. "You're not riding track, Lola, that's final."

I was going to tell him that I'd breezed Ginger the other day, but I wasn't sure whether this would convince him to let me ride, or get me into more trouble. As it turned out, I didn't need to argue because Nonna stepped up to take my side.

"You should let her ride, Ray," she said gently. "Lola is a good rider, she's ready for it. Besides, what else is she going to do? Sit around the house all day?"

"She can stay home and hit the books, that's what she can do," my dad replied. "You don't become a doctor by racing horses around a track."

"I don't want to be a doctor," I mumbled.

My dad looked hard at me. "Lola, you know what Mr Azzaretti told me? He said you're the brightest kid in his whole school and if you maintain your grade point average like it is now, you would have the choice of any college you want. You could be a doctor or a lawyer or an astronaut, or the President of the United States, but the one thing you're not going to be is a jockey. Do you understand me?"

"I didn't realise being bright would get me punishment," I said.

"That's a lot of backchat for a girl who just got suspended," my dad replied. And I knew I had pushed him too far.

There was no point in getting up early the next day, but I was out of bed by six anyway, and I had all my study done by midday. There was nothing else to do except watch TV. Our TV room had a big overstuffed sofa and I was curled up on it watching a reality show on repeat when Nonna came in.

"Where's the remote?" She began hunting under the magazines on the coffee table. She looked anxious, which was unlike her.

"Here, Nonna." I had it under my cushion.

She took it from me and switched the TV to the racing channel.

"Race six at Churchill Downs," the commentator was saying. "The three-year-old maiden stakes. And the horses are heading into the start gates now…"

"There she is." Nonna nodded at the screen. "Number four in the yellow and green silks. What do you think, Lola?"

I looked at the horse with the number four on her saddle blanket. She was a big bay with two white hind socks.

"That's Aces High?" I asked. "The horse that you wouldn't let Dad bet on?"

"That's her," Nonna confirmed.

I looked hard at the TV screen.

"I don't know," I said. "It's hard to tell without seeing her in real life."

"That's right," Nonna said. "You've got to be able to look them in the eye, Loretta."

She had called me by my full name – Loretta – which she never usually did. I had been named after her, but most of the time everyone in the house called me Lola to avoid confusion. I figured it was because Nonna was so busy focusing on the horses, she wasn't thinking straight.

"I've seen this filly up close when she was stabled here at Aqueduct and she is very special," Nonna told me, staring at the TV. "When she steps out onto the track you cannot take your eyes off her. She's got perfect conformation. The best I've ever seen. And powerful too for such a young horse…"

The commentator had been reeling off facts and figures about the horses in the field and now I heard him say the filly's name. "Aces High is going into the start gates now. She's a well-bred filly who got started at Frankie Di Marco's stables in Ozone Park, New York before she was brought here to Kentucky…"

"Look at the muscle!" Nonna Loretta said. "Lance must have been doing hillwork to build up her hindquarters. She's even better than I remember her."

I wondered why Nonna Loretta cared so much. After all, she'd told Dad point-blank that he couldn't bet on the filly.

"They're off!" The commentator's voice barked out from the TV as the barriers opened. Suddenly I felt sick with nerves, although I didn't quite know why.

"*Andare!* Aces High!" Nonna shouted. "*Andare! Andare!*"

She was still yelling at the TV in Italian as the

horses swept around the first furlong marker. I could see Aces High halfway up in the pack, pinned in by the railings.

"She needs to get out wide so she can make a move," I said.

Nonna shook her head. "She's sitting just fine where she is for now. That filly is a stayer. She has a strong finish in her."

The fourth furlong marker was the halfway point in the race and by then the horses that had taken the early lead were flagging a little, but Aces High looked like she was cruising along. She was still boxed in by the railing though, and now Nonna looked worried.

"What is that *ragazzo* on her back doing?" Nonna was clasping her hands together anxiously. "He needs to move now! *Andare!*"

And then it happened. It was as if the jockey had heard my nonna's instructions through the television because suddenly he made his move. Not to the outside as I expected, but closer to the rail. A gap opened up there and he saw it and took his chance. With a quick wave of his whip near the filly's face just to show her it was time to go, he asked her to step up the pace and she responded instantly, surging forward. She was so quick to accelerate that if you didn't have your eyes on her you would have missed the moment. I saw the flash of brilliance as she lengthened out and began to move and with three quick strides she had slipped through the hole and was powering ahead of the two horses who'd had her boxed-in just moments before. Then she had overtaken them both and was in the clear. There were only three horses in front of her now and three furlongs to go.

"Go, Aces High!" I was screaming at the TV. "Go!"

It was like those other horses were standing still, the way her strides ate up the ground between them, closing the gap, passing the horse in front of her and then the next one until there was just one horse ahead of her coming into the home straight.

"You can do it!" My nonna had her hands clasped together as if she was praying. I was jumping up and down like crazy. "Go! Go! Go!"

"Look at this filly coming up the inside!" the commentator was shouting. "She's taking it all the way home! Aces High has taken the lead and at the finish post it is Aces High by a full length! Aces High wins the Maiden!"

Nonna Loretta fell strangely silent. She was still staring at the screen.

I heard the front door slam. And then Dad entered the room. His face was flushed with anger. He saw the TV screen.

"You were watching that?" he asked Nonna. He looked like he was going to burst a vein in his forehead. "I heard the whole thing on the car radio. I told you, Loretta! I told you! She won the race just like I said she would! If it weren't for you…"

"If it wasn't for me," Nonna finished his sentence for him, "then we wouldn't have just won seventy-three thousand dollars."

Dad was stunned. "What are you talking about?"

On the TV screen Aces High was being led into the winner's enclosure and a wreath of roses was being draped around her neck. Nonna couldn't take her eyes off her. "I bet on the horse," she said. "One thousand dollars at seventy-three to one."

"You did what?" My dad was confused. "Where

did you get a thousand dollars?"

"I pawned the jewellery," Nonna said, still staring at the TV. "My rings…"

My dad looked at her in total disbelief. "You told me that I couldn't bet. You said it was the rules…"

"Oh, Raymond," Nonna said calmly. "Those rules are for you – not for me!"

She ignored his speechless wonder and turned to me.

"Lola," she said. "I was wondering… since you have no school right now, how would you like to take a trip with me next week?"

"A trip, Nonna?" I said. "Where are we going?"

"We're going home," she said.

"Home?"

"Yes." She had a look in her eye like a kid gets at Christmas time.

"Home to Italy."

The Villa

Our house in Ozone Park was so close to JFK airport that I could look out of my bedroom window at night and see the plane lights above me in the sky.

Now I was one of those lights, shining in the inky darkness above the city.

"Lola." Nonna clasped my hand as she peered out from the window seat. "Look how big it is. It goes on for ever!"

Nonna had never seen New York from above before.

"When I arrived from Italy, I came by boat," she told me. "I remember I had just enough money to buy a third class berth. The meals were free, thank goodness, because I didn't have any money left for food.

"When I got off the boat at Ellis Island they asked me all these questions and I was so scared they would put me on the boat straight back to Italy again, but I was strong and healthy and I could speak a little English, so even though I didn't have a cent to take care of myself they let me through."

"Were you all alone?" I asked. I knew the answer to this question before I even asked it. Nonna had told me the tale of how she arrived in New York many times. But I loved the story and I made her tell it again and again, always prompting her in the right places.

"I didn't know a soul," Nonna confirmed. "And I had no idea where to go. New York was a very big city, even back then. I asked the man at the immigration counter where I could find horses. Well, he said I should go to Aqueduct because it was the finest racetrack on the East Coast and right here in this very city!

"You wouldn't have recognised it, Lola. Aqueduct was a beautiful place back in those days, so elegant!

All the stables were brand new and on race days everyone in the grandstand was dressed in their best clothes like ladies and gentlemen.

"I went down to the stables and I asked around for horses to ride, but they were shocked that a sixteen-year-old girl wanted to be a jockey. None of the trainers would employ me. So I took the only job I could get, at the clubhouse as a waitress. On my first day, in front of everyone, I dropped a whole tray and all the cutlery and the coffee cups went flying and this nice young man bent down and helped me pick it all up. He introduced himself as Alberto and that was how I met your grandfather."

"Was he working there too?" I asked.

"No," Nonna said. "He was an apprentice jockey. We got to talking and he told me they needed someone to ride trackwork at his yard. He took me to the stables and gave me some silks to wear. We tucked my hair out of the way so that no one knew I was a girl and I mounted up on this big bay Thoroughbred and rode out on the track like I'd been doing it all my life. The head trainer saw me ride and it didn't matter that I was a girl any more, he gave me the job…"

"Ma'am?" It was the flight attendant. "Would you like a cup of tea or coffee?"

Nonna looked up at her. "Young lady," she said. "How long is this flight going to take?"

"New York to Rome is eight hours exactly, ma'am," the young woman said.

My nonna looked amazed. "It took thirteen days last time!"

"When was that, ma'am?"

"1945," Nonna replied. "I haven't been home since."

The attendant smiled at me. "And is this your granddaughter, ma'am?"

"Yes," Nonna replied. "Do you know she's never been to Italy before?"

"I've never been anywhere before, Nonna," I pointed out.

"Are you staying in Rome?"

"Oh no!" Nonna said. "Rome is too busy – a crazy place. We're going to my town, to Siena. Have you been there?"

"No," the attendant replied. "But I hear it's very beautiful."

"It is. The most beautiful place in the world," Nonna said softly, and I felt her grip tighten, like a child who suddenly panics and strengthens their hold on their mom's hand at the edge of a busy intersection.

"It has been a very long time since I went home, Lola," she murmured.

The attendant brought me an orange juice and a little bag with two tiny sweet biscuits as well. I wanted to eat them, but I decided to put them in my bag to take home. I had kept my boarding pass too. I was gathering souvenirs. I couldn't believe that I was actually going to Italy. Mostly I couldn't believe that Dad had agreed to let me go.

Dad is overprotective of me. Nonna says it's understandable because I was only four when Mom died. But I've always had Nonna to look after me.

Dad refused at first, but Nonna wore him down. "Why not?" Nonna said. "Lola's got no school. What else is she doing for the next month, Ray?"

"That's not the point," my dad said.

"Why can't Nonna take me too?" Donna whined.

"Don't you get involved!" my dad snapped. "Anyway, you've got beauty school exams."

Donna glared at me. "I don't see why Lola gets to go. She gets suspended from school – and her punishment is a trip to Italy?"

"Lola is coming to help take care of me," Nonna said. "I need a companion."

"Loretta." My dad rolled his eyes. "You don't need anyone to take care of you!"

"I'm an 85-year-old woman," Nonna shot back. "And you want to send me off halfway across the world on my own?"

"Mom," said my dad, sighing. "What's the hurry all of a sudden? Why don't you wait? We can all go together. It'll be a family holiday, maybe at Christmas…"

"Christmas is too far away when you are my age, Raymond," Nonna said. "Besides, we can't all go at once. You know someone has to stay with the horses."

Dad began to grumble, but Nonna was stubborn, there was no way she was changing her mind. "All

I want is this one last journey home," she told him. "And I want my Piccolina to come with me."

I am a New York kid, so all the people and traffic didn't make much of an impression on me. Rome was just another busy city like back home. What knocked me out though was how pretty it all was, all the monuments and statues. Everywhere you looked there were sculptures of naked gods and chariots and horses, some as big as buildings, made out of smooth grey stone.

I stared out the window at the gods as we drove to the railway station. Nonna was rattling off instructions to the cab driver, her hands waving wildly. I can speak a little Italian, but Nonna talked so fast I couldn't make out a word. At the station she hustled us through the crowd, bought our tickets and guided us through the terminal and onto the right train. That first train took us through the dingy suburban outskirts of the city and then we were clear of the buildings and in the countryside. Two hours later we changed to a different train and soon the view became nothing but rows of grape vines and hillsides of olive trees zipping by.

By now we had been travelling for almost a whole day and I had barely slept so I was exhausted. The jetlag made me feel weird, too, like there was an ocean tide inside me, ebbing back and forth, making me almost seasick. By the time we got off the train at Siena and into a taxi I could barely keep my eyes open.

"Are you sleepy, Piccolina?" Nonna gave me a cuddle. "Don't worry, we are almost there…"

I must have fallen asleep in the taxi because the next thing I knew, Nonna was shaking me softly by the shoulder.

"Piccolina, wake up… We're here."

I opened my eyes. We were in the middle of an olive grove, bumping along a narrow gravel driveway. Ahead of us, I could see a row of tall conifers forming a sentry, and as we drove past them our destination came into view.

It was an old stone villa, two storeys high, with shutters on the windows and overgrown yellow roses smothering the arch of the front doorway.

"Is this a hotel?" I asked.

"No, Lola." Nonna Loretta's voice was quiet. "This is my home. My family have owned this land for centuries."

"You used to live here?" I peered out the taxi window at the villa. It looked kind of rundown. "Who lives here now?"

"Nobody," Nonna said. "It's been empty a long time."

Nonna got me to lift our suitcases from the trunk while she counted out money for the cab driver. They were speaking Italian and I think they must have argued about the tip because he barely waited for me to get the last bag out before driving away, dust flying up from his tyres.

"Look underneath the geranium, Lola," Nonna instructed, pointing to the bright red flower in the terracotta pot on the doorstep. "The key should be there."

I tilted the pot. There was the key, just like Nonna said: black iron, covered in dirt.

I held it out to her, but Nonna shook her head, almost like she was reluctant to touch it.

"You do it, Piccolina."

The door was arched, made of solid wood with these big wrought iron hinges, like an old-fashioned gaol. I put the key in and tried to turn it.

"It doesn't fit," I said. I felt like we were breaking into someone's house. But if it wasn't her house then how did Nonna know where the key would be?

"You have to jiggle it in the lock to make it work sometimes," Nonna said.

"It must have been locked up for a long time," I said.

"It has," Nonna agreed. "No one has lived here since my mama died."

I had just about given up on making the key work when something in the lock clicked, the key turned at last and the door swung open.

You know how a jewel box will look quite plain on the outside and then you open it up and there is a shock of pink silk? The villa was like that. All grey stone outside, but when I opened that door the sunlight flooded in on an entranceway full of colour. The floors were patterned in the most brilliant blue and turquoise Moroccan tiles and to the left the tiles continued up the staircase where the wall had been painted emerald green with a mural of a giant tree, tangles of black branches covered in pink roses spreading out in every direction all the way to the landing. The other walls downstairs were painted in a mind-bending harlequin pattern of brilliant orange, black and white diamonds, although the pattern was barely visible because of all the oil paintings hung on top. There were loads of them – all different sizes, some in gilt frames and others in plain wood. They were daubed in thick, richly coloured oil paint and nearly all of them were of horses. In between the paintings there were framed black and white photographs, also of horses. A massive glass trophy case filled up most of the back wall, its shelves crammed with even more photographs, rosettes and tarnished silver cups and trophies and medals.

There were swords crossed on the wall beside it, real ones, and at the foot of the stairs a suit of armour stood sentry draped in an orange, black and white flag.

"Nonna! Are you serious? Look at this place! Is this really your home?"

Nonna didn't reply. I looked for her and realised she hadn't entered the house. She was still standing on the doorstep, as if some invisible force held her back.

"Nonna?" I walked towards her and took her hand. She squeezed her fingers tight around mine and then she took a deep breath and stepped across the threshold.

"I haven't stood in this room for almost seventy years," she said looking around in amazement, "and yet it is all the same, just as I remember. A little smaller maybe…"

She let go of my hand and walked straight up to the suit of armour so that she was standing face to face with it, raised her tiny fist, knocked on the helmet then prised the visor open. "Good day, Donatello, I am home!" she said.

She turned to me with a smile. "My brother tried to climb inside him once when we were very little and got his head stuck. We had to use olive oil on Donatello to get him out. Mama was furious!"

"Donatello was your brother?" I asked.

Nonna Loretta laughed. "Donatello is the armour!

My brother's name was Carlo."

I knew Nonna had a brother, but she had never said his name before. She hardly ever said anything about her family. She loved to tell stories, my nonna, but they always began from the day she arrived in New York with her duffel bag at Ellis Island. Whenever I asked her about her old life in Italy she had always claimed that she was too young to remember any of it.

"It is lost in the mists," she would say dismissively if I pestered her. "Who can remember what happened so many years ago? And what does it matter anyway?"

The one thing I knew for sure about Nonna's brother was that he had died in the war. My dad told me once that Nonna was very sad about her brother's death and that was the real reason why she never liked to talk about Italy.

Nonna creaked the visor shut on Donatello and rearranged the flag that was draped over his shoulder. Then she turned to me. "Fetch the suitcases would you, Piccolina?" she said.

I struggled up the stairs with our luggage, stopping

on the landing to drop the bags and rest. Up close, the painted tree was slightly terrifying, the way the tangle of black branches seemed to reach out of the wall to grab at you.

"Was this picture on the wall when you lived here?" I asked.

"The tree?" Nonna said. "Yes, my mama painted it. It is strange, when I look at it I can feel her presence so strong, even though she is gone."

"What was she like?" I asked.

"Oh, you know, she was my mama," Nonna said, as if that explained everything.

"Was she an artist?"

"She was good with her hands, painting and cooking and sewing. She cared very much for Carlo and me, but she was a very opinionated woman and obstinate too…" Nonna gave a chuckle. "I could be speaking of myself, couldn't I? Perhaps that is where I get it from!"

Upstairs the paint along the hallway had begun to flake off and the plaster beneath it was crumbling. A thick layer of dust covered everything. We would have to get the place cleaned up, but at least it was liveable. Nonna opened the linen cupboard and began to pull out pillows and duvets from under a dust sheet, while I washed in the bathroom and discovered that the taps only ran cold and not hot water because there was no electricity.

"You will have my old bedroom," Nonna told me. It was the first one at the top of the landing, with walls painted in dusky pink with crimson stripes. The budding bough of a tree bloomed out of one corner of the room and a white peacock perched on the bough with its tail spread out beneath it.

"Mama painted it pink with stripes and then I asked her to add the tree and the peacock," Nonna said. "She never got the peacock quite right. You see how his head is too big?"

"It's amazing," I said. "It must have been the most incredible house to grow up in."

"It was," Nonna said. "I was very happy here." But her eyes didn't look happy at all. They were shining with tears.

"I'll fetch you another blanket. You must be tired, Piccolina," she murmured. "We'll make the bed up and you can get some sleep."

The jetlag that had begun to set in at the train station was like nothing I had ever felt before and despite the fact that it was still light outside I was suddenly too exhausted to stay awake any longer.

I must have fallen asleep thinking about that mural above the stairs, because in my dreams I was walking through a forest, only the trees weren't real, they were painted ones, and when their black branches touched my skin they clung to me like seaweed. I was trying to navigate my way through when I realised that I wasn't alone. There was something in the woods, stalking me. I began pushing my way through the trees, my heart pounding, and the creature sensed my fear and gave chase. I could hear it crashing through the undergrowth right behind me and I was running, but it was like my legs were stuck in treacle, a low animal growl growing louder, gaining with every stride.

I looked back over my shoulder, hoping that I would see nothing, but the creature was right there, monstrous and bristling, cold grey eyes fixed on me.

It was a wolf. A female with two little cubs at her feet. They followed her obediently, although she ignored them because her focus was completely on me.

I ran harder, my breath coming in frantic gasps. The grey wolf was gaining, I could hear her closing in, smell the hot animal stench of her.

Suddenly, in the middle of the forest, a stone building rose up right in front of me and I had to turn so fast to stop from running into it that I fell. I dropped to my knees on the ground which I realised was not a forest floor at all but hard, cold tiles, the same as the turquoise and blue ones downstairs. I was trying to get up again when the wolf leapt on top of me. She knocked me flat to the floor, sprawling me out on my back, her paws on my chest pinning me down and her great, grey menacing head hanging over my face so that I could see the saliva dripping from her teeth.

And then she spoke.

"Loyal are the people of the Wolf. Bravest of all the seventeen," she growled. She came closer so that I could smell her fetid breath on my face. "You will need to run faster than this to win little one. You must prove yourself worthy to bring home the banner."

She was crushing me. I could feel this enormous weight on my chest and I struggled with all my might to get her off me. I was shouting and screaming and the branches were alive and tangling around me. Then I realised they were not branches at all but bedsheets and I opened my eyes. The wolf was gone and I was wide-awake and starving.

Daredevil

I looked in all the cupboards downstairs but of course there was no food in the house.

"You'll have to go into town, Lola," Nonna said. "It's not far from here – about twenty minutes' walk."

She took out a pen and a piece of paper from her handbag. "Here is the road." Nonna drew me a map. "You go along until you see a small stream with a narrow bridge over it, and then you turn the corner and go over another bridge and you reach an avenue of tall trees… they take you to an arched gateway called Porta Ovile."

She sketched the city walls around the archway with crenellations on top of it like a castle. "Behind the high walls follow your nose through the streets and you'll reach the piazza. There's a marketplace with stalls selling fruit and bread and cheese. You can buy us food there."

"Nonna," I said. "You haven't lived here for seventy years. I don't think there's still going to be a market stall in the same place there was when you were a girl."

Nonna chuckled. "Ah, Lola, you don't understand Italy." She dug in her purse and handed me some money. "Hundreds of years go by and nothing changes here."

She closed my hand around the money and the map. "Get the small black olives please. They are tastier than the large ones."

As I walked along the road in the afternoon sun I wondered if I would be able to make a map of Ozone Park in seventy years' time. I doubted it. Things changed faster in New York. There was a Dunkin' Donuts on the corner of Rockaway that wasn't there even a couple of months ago.

The morning sun was baking hot already and my legs were overheating in my jeans. Up ahead of me, over the crest of the hill, I could make out an avenue shaded by plane trees, and beyond the trees the walls of the city rose up to the sky. Further down the avenue there was a wide archway almost three storeys high in the wall. I stood in front of it and read the words written into the bricks at the top: Porta Ovile.

Through the archway the broad cobbled street split off in three directions. I took the middle road, which soon narrowed until it was crushed into an alleyway by the ancient buildings on both sides. Nonna had told me to follow my nose, but my nose was hopelessly lost. I was in a labyrinth where every turn I took looked exactly the same.

When I went down a side alley that was just like all the rest it came as a surprise to reach the corner and see that I was actually there, in the piazza.

The way Nonna had talked about the piazza I thought it would be tiny, but in fact it was this enormous open space. Tall brick buildings encircled the perimeter of the square, looming on every side so that it seemed as if they were holding back the sky, an effect that was made more dramatic because the red bricks that paved the floor of the piazza swooped away and sloped down to the marble staircase at the base of a very grand building, which I guessed must be the town hall.

The side of the piazza where I had emerged was shaded by the buildings, but on the upper half there were market stalls still bathed in sunlight. Tables with white linen cloths on them were piled with fresh baked bread, bottles of olive oil, red wine, cheese, meats and punnets of fresh raspberries and blackberries. The busiest stall was an ice-cream stand with chillers piled high with snowy whipped peaks of gelato.

At the first stall selling cheeses the old lady shopkeeper began to chat away to me merrily in Italian and I suddenly felt shy about speaking with my New York accent and getting the words wrong, so my shopping technique became a silent game of smile-and-point. I travelled from stall to stall, getting raspberries and cheese and oil until my bag was full. *Grazie, grazie, grazie.*

If all the streets had looked the same on the way in, it was worse finding my way out. I tried to find a familiar signpost, but the names meant nothing to me. Via Caterina, Via del Paradiso… Finally I chose one at random and followed that for a while. When it branched into two directions I found myself on a street that seemed strangely familiar, the Via di Vallerozzi. My confidence in my sense of direction began to fade when I realised that the street was not a main avenue, in fact it was totally deserted. Was this the right way? I continued on, trying not to trip on the cobbles, keeping a tight grip on the groceries in my arms.

That was when I heard the song. It was this old Italian opera song and I recognised it because Nonna always sang it when she was cleaning the house, but this was a man's voice singing it. I couldn't see anyone at first but as I got further down the street there was this grey-haired old man, with his head bent down over a bed of white roses that were planted around the edge of a fountain. He was focused on his work and singing loudly to himself as he gardened, his bony hands using a pair of wiry garden scissors to trim the dead leaves away.

"Excuse me?" I said. "Sorry. Do you know how to

get to the Porta Ovile from here?"

The old man straightened up and turned to me. I smiled at him, but he didn't smile back. I figured he mustn't understand English and tried again in Italian. "*Scusi?*" I pointed up the street. "Porta Ovile?"

The old man was staring, looking at me hard. The way his eyes examined me really creeped me out.

"*Lo ti conosco…*" he said.

I know you.

"No," I shook my head. "No, you don't know me. I just need directions. Do you speak English?"

"*Lo ti conosco…*" he said it again firmly. He took off his glasses and wiped them, blinked and put them on again.

He was just flat-out inspecting me as if I were a museum exhibit or something! Then his eyes widened, as if a memory had been triggered. "*Lo ti conosco…*" He stepped forward and I stepped back, moving away from him.

"Never mind…" I began but then he pointed at me and started shouting.

"*Scavezzecolla!*" he cried. "*Scavezzecolla!*"

Little bits of spittle formed at the corners of his mouth as he spat out the words. It was like I'd done something wrong – I didn't know what he was going on about. "*Scavezzecolla!*" He stretched his arms out and began to come at me.

"Hey! Watch it!" I backed away. The crazy old man still had his scissors in his hand!

"*Scavezzecolla! Attesa!*"

Attesa! I knew that word. Wait! Was he serious? No way. I turned and started to jog down the street, my groceries banging up and down inside the bag in my arms. I looked around for help but there was no one else in the street.

"*Scavezzecolla! Scavezzecolla!*"

He was coming after me!

"Leave me alone!" I yelled back at him. "Go away you crazy old man!"

"*Attesa!*"

I could hear him hobbling after me across the cobbles. "*Scavezzecolla!*"

That was when I ran.

By the time I reached the Porta Ovile I couldn't see him behind me any more. My legs were shaking but I kept running, all the way back, until I arrived at last, panting and terrified, at the villa.

I worked the rusty old key in the lock.

"Come on! Open!" I wrenched it until it turned and then ran inside and slammed the door behind me.

I dropped my shopping bag to the floor and ran across to the windows and peered out. There was no one there. He hadn't followed me.

"Lola?" My grandmother came out from the kitchen. "Did you…"

Then she saw the state I was in.

"What happened?"

"I got chased," I said.

"What?"

"There was this old man. I asked him for directions home and he came at me with a pair of scissors!"

"What?"

"He was crazy! He chased me all the way down the street!"

"Where did you see him?"

"Outside a big red-brick building. He was trimming the roses by a fountain in the Via di

Vallerozzi. He was shouting at me! He kept saying this word "*Scavezzecolla! Scavezzecolla!*"

My grandmother had suddenly turned pale.

"Nonna? Are you OK?"

She looked like she was about to faint. Her hand reached out for support, gripping at the stair rail.

I ran to the kitchen and grabbed her a wooden chair. She slumped into the seat and I stood and watched the colour return to her cheeks.

"I'm all right, Piccolina," she breathed. "It's just…Well, I haven't heard that word in a very long time."

Nonna didn't say anything more for a moment. Then she reached out and grasped my hand so that she could stand up again.

"Come on, Piccolina," she said. "I want to show you something."

I had taken a glimpse into the trophy cabinet in the hallway when we first arrived. It was filled with rosettes, silver salvers, medals and old photographs, most of them of horses. There was one photo that I hadn't noticed behind the trophies. Nonna reached into the cabinet and pulled it out so that I could see it properly. It was a horse, a pretty black mare with a star on her forehead, held by a young girl dressed in a floral rosebud dress with her hair swept back off her face. She was smiling broadly and looking straight at the camera. I stared at the picture in wonder. The girl in the photograph was me!

"Isn't it silly?" Nonna smiled. "I was so self-conscious about my looks back then – I never realised at the time how beautiful I was."

"This girl in the photo – it's you?"

"Yes, Lola," Nonna said. "I must have been fifteen when the picture was taken so I was three years older than you are, but we look very similar, don't we?"

She gave a cackle of delight. "That old the man on the Via di Vallerozzi must have thought he was seeing a ghost."

"So he thought I was you?"

Nonna nodded. "He hasn't forgotten what happened all those years ago. Well, let him see ghosts, I say. The past has haunted me for long enough, it is his turn now."

"You know him?" I said.

"Yes," Nonna said. "His name is Alonzo de

Monte and he is the Prior. I have not seen him in seventy years."

"Well," I said, "I think he's still angry at you for something."

Nonna laughed. "Yes, it seems that he is. He is the most powerful man in the contrada and the feelings run strong in him."

"Contrada?"

"Seventeen contradas to symbolise the seventeen districts of Siena. Each one had its own symbol – there are the Forest and the Tower but most are named after animals. The Unicorn, the Tortoise and the Eagle, and our most hated enemies, the Contrada of Istrice – the Porcupine.

"What was your contrada?" I asked.

Nonna gazed up at the coat of arms on the wall, a shield painted in orange, black and white. In the middle of the shield was a creature with bared fangs and cold grey eyes.

"Lupa," Nonna said. "The She-Wolf. Bravest of all the seventeen."

Bravest of all the seventeen.

The words that the wolf had spoken in my dream.

"You belong to the Wolf?"

"I did. But not any more," Nonna replied. "The Via di Vallerozzi where you walked today is home of the Lupa. It is the boundary of the contrada. Back in my day you did not dare cross the street and enter another contrada, such was our dislike for each other."

"You mean like how kids from Ozone Park hate the rich kids from Jamaica Hills?"

"Not like that at all." Nonna shook her head. "This is not just a playground squabble, a few stones thrown in the street. This is serious. The contrada is life and death. For hundreds of years the seventeen have been arch rivals and they hate each other with such a passion, like nothing you have ever seen. In ancient times battles were fought and armies were raised as the contradas each tried to prove their greatness. Then, as the years passed by, the contest between the clans became a race. That race, the Palio, is hailed as the greatest and most dangerous horse race in the world, held every year in the streets of the piazza."

"The piazza?" I was confused. "But I've seen the

piazza. It's in the middle of the town, with buildings all around it and it's on a slope, paved in brick."

"That's what makes it so dangerous," Nonna said. "The horses race three times around the square and there are many crashes as riders fail to make the treacherous turns in time. It is even harder because they must ride bareback."

"They don't use saddles?"

"Saddles are forbidden," Nonna said. "But it is not against the rules to kick or push or throw a punch. It is a very vicious race, and there is so much to lose. A Palio jockey must be fearless. The best ones, the most famous, earn themselves nicknames to match their nature. In my day there was *Barbaro* – the barbarian. Oh that man he rode like a brute, punching and whipping other riders to force them off the track! And *Subdolo* – the sneaky one – he would come up behind you and just like that he would steal the lead! The worst was *Il Prepotente* – the bully – he was a very dangerous opponent, he would barge you into walls and cut you off and leave you for dead."

Nonna looked down at the photo in her hands.

"They called me *Scavezzecolla*. It means the daredevil. They used to say I would take risks no other rider would dare, riding for the smallest of gaps and never slowing down."

"You raced in the Palio?" I said. "Nonna, why didn't you ever tell me?"

Nonna shrugged. "I told you that I used to ride."

"You never told me anything about this!"

"Lola, it was such a long time ago, does it matter now?"

"Yes!" I insisted. "It matters because whatever happened back then is still so important that an old man chased me through the streets today thinking that I was you!"

"The Prior?" Nonna harrumphed. "The Palio is everything to him. It always has been. Even when there was a war on and people were dying, all he could think about was winning that stupid, stupid race…"

Nonna's eyes were shining with tears, her hands trembling as they held the photograph.

"I'm sorry, Nonna," I said. "I didn't mean to upset you."

Gently, I took the photo from her and wiped the dust from the frame and put it back in the cabinet. "Come on. I bought coffee at the market, why don't you sit down in the kitchen and I will brew you a cup?"

Nonna still looked shaken but she managed to give me a weak smile. "All right, Lola," she said. "Yes, coffee would be nice."

Together we went into the kitchen and while she sat down at the table I made the coffee. I added an extra teaspoon of sugar to give her energy. She looked so exhausted.

"I am the one who is sorry, Lola," she said as I handed the coffee to her. "I shouldn't have got so upset. And you are right, I should have warned you. I thought I was ready to return and face my past but the pain of it all is so deep I wonder if it is best to forget it all and go home again…"

"No," I said. "You are stronger than that, Nonna. We didn't come all this way to turn back just because of one stupid old man."

I sat down at the table beside her and took her hand. "But I need to know. Please, Nonna. All of it.

About the Palio and what happened to you. Will you tell me?"

Nonna gave a wan smile.

"Very well, Piccolina," she said. "But I must start at the beginning because this story is not only about me, it is also about my brother, Carlo, and of course Stella."

"Stella? Who was she? Your sister?"

"No," Nonna said. "Stella was my horse."

Carlo the Fantino

I always think of Stella as my horse, but in truth she belonged to Carlo. She loved Carlo with all her heart – but then all the horses loved my big brother. He had the best instincts of any horseman I have ever met. At our farm he was responsible for breaking in the young wild ones and he never once got thrown off. My papa would say that Carlo was so skilled he "could tame a hurricane and ride the wind".

Stella was a hurricane on four legs. She was born in the fields beside our farm. Her mother was one of our best racing horses, an Anglo-Arab mare with excellent bloodlines. The mare was put to stud with a famous stallion called Titan. But when Stella was born jet-black we suspected the handsome chestnut could not have been her father after all. So we never knew for sure who her real sire was.

Regardless of her bloodlines she was a beauty, with these big wide eyes and a perfect white mark on her forehead from which she took her name – Stella. It means star. I loved her from the moment I saw her, but it was Carlo that she adored. Stella would follow Carlo around the fields and chase him in a game of tag as if he were a horse too. By the time she was old enough to be backed and ridden, their bond was so close that it seemed the most natural thing in the world for Carlo to climb on her back and gallop her across the fields without a saddle or bridle.

We all rode without saddles. There were plenty of them in the tack room, but Papa said that it was better to train without them. Our horses were all intended for the Palio and the race had to be ridden bareback so it was vital that we should develop the ability to grip onto a slippery horse at full gallop.

We were a racing family for many generations. The Palio was in our blood, so it was destiny that Carlo would ride in it. He rode his first Palio when he was fifteen and won it by almost two lengths, leading from start to finish. His second Palio was much harder fought. His horse, Serafina, was slow to start and they had to battle their way through as just about every rider on the course colluded to try to stop them. The Wolf contrada has a great many enemies and in the Palio these enemies are determined to destroy you, even if it means forfeiting their chance to win.

Carlo had to endure the kicks and punches of the jockeys as he pushed past them and drove Serafina on to the finish line, but despite all their efforts to beat him he was too good and for a second time in a row, he won.

The year that followed was 1940. As the Palio drew near, the Capitano, who is in charge of all preparations for the race, announced that for the third year in a row Carlo would be the fantino – the jockey who would ride for the Contrada of the Wolf. No one would dare to disagree with the Capitano – and besides, the whole contrada agreed my brother was the best rider by far and would ensure that once again the Wolf would claim victory.

Everywhere that Carlo went, the people would whisper "Fantino" with admiration. He was a handsome boy with black curly hair and soft grey eyes and small white teeth and the girls threw themselves at him. To be the girlfriend of the fantino was considered very glamorous – like the girls today who dream of marrying professional footballers.

It wasn't just the girls he was popular with. If Mama sent him to the market, Carlo would return home with all sorts of things that she had never asked for, such as olives and cheese, without having spent a cent because the stallholders lavished gifts on him.

As the Palio approached, Carlo and I began to train the horses. Stella was still too young for him to ride in the race and he had decided that once again he would be riding Serafina. The bay mare was seven years old – a good age to race. For fitness we would take her out into the hills around Siena. I would ride Stella and Carlo would be on Serafina. Most of the time we would trot, going long distances into the high hills to build up their muscles and stamina. I remember that day, the way Carlo kept insisting that we trot when I wanted to gallop.

"We're supposed to be training for a race," I complained.

"You want to ruin their tendons by pushing the horses before they are ready?" he shot back.

"You are so boring!" I teased him. "Come on! Let's go! I'll give you a head start and... hey!"

Carlo was gone. He had leapt forward at a gallop on Serafina and was already two lengths ahead.

"You cheat!" I shouted after him. "Is this how you win

the Palio?" I urged Stella to chase after them and the black mare responded instantly and broke straight into a gallop. Carlo and Serafina already had a good four lengths' head start.

"We'll catch you by the top of the hill!" I shouted after him into the wind.

The climb was steep and halfway up the hill I felt Stella starting to flag beneath me. "You can do it!" I urged her to gallop on, and when she responded despite her tiredness, I felt the power in her. Her strides began to open up, devouring the ground, and by the time we came around the next corner where the road twisted again she was stretched out flat at a gallop and I was certain we were going to beat Carlo and Serafina.

"We'll catch them on the next hill," I murmured to Stella as I watched my brother and his horse disappear around the bend ahead of us. And then we came around the corner and suddenly I was pulling hard on the reins to avoid colliding with Carlo and Serafina who had stopped in the middle of the road.

A big black car was parked sideways, blocking the way through. Carlo had come to a halt in front of it, dismounted, and was talking to a man beside the car.

I had never met the man before. He had taken his hat off and was totally bald with a thick, bull neck that seemed to sprout into his face. His nose was squashed flat, like he'd been punched many times in a fight, and his mouth turned down at the edges in a permanent frown.

"What is going on?" I asked. "Move your car!"

"Young lady." The man put up a hand to silence me. "If you could go away and give us a moment, please? I need to talk alone with your brother."

"No!" I said.

The man was taken aback. "It will just be a moment, it is very important."

I scowled at him. "Who are you anyway? Were you waiting here for us? I nearly hurt my horse because of you and..."

"Loretta!" Carlo silenced me. Then in a softer voice he said. "It's OK, kid. Take the horses and walk them for a bit so that they cool down. This won't take long."

Reluctantly I did as Carlo asked, taking both horses and walking them in long loops up and down the hill road, all the while keeping an eye on my brother and the strange bald man.

The man was doing most of the talking. He was gesturing

vigorously, his hands opened out warmly to Carlo. My brother didn't say anything. His face was a mask. He stood and listened for ages. Then, at last, he spoke and whatever he said turned the man's face puce with anger. The man's gestures became furious. He was punching at the air right in front of Carlo. Carlo didn't flinch as the fists came inches in front of his face. He shook his head and then he turned and walked away.

"You are making a mistake!" the man yelled after him. "You will be sorry for this!"

"Come on, Loretta," my brother said, taking back Serafina's reins and mounting up. "Let's get out of here."

"What was all that about?" I looked over my shoulder at the man who was stomping back to his car.

"He is the Prior from the Contrada of the Istrice," Carlo said. "He came here today to bribe me."

"He wanted you to swap teams and ride for him?" I asked.

"No." Carlo curled his lip in disgust. "Worse. He wanted me to cheat, to lose on purpose and throw the race. He offered me a lot of money. And when I said no, he threatened to have his rider break my legs in the race."

I was horrified. "Carlo! We must tell the police!"

My brother laughed. "Loretta," he said. "This is the Palio. Bribery and threats are part of the game. Do you not think the police officer will have a favourite contrada that he too wants to win?"

"But I don't want anyone to break your legs!" I said.

"No one is going to get anywhere near me, so how can they break my legs?" Carlo said. "Don't worry, Loretta. This is the usual pre-race stuff. A load of nonsense if you ask me! Why do people get so worked up about a horse race?"

There was the roar of a car engine and our horses both spooked a little as the black car skidded close by us, and the Prior of the Istrice contrada drove at breakneck speed back down the hill.

"The people of the Porcupine are taking things too far this time," I said.

"Loretta, the people of our own contrada are no different," Carlo said. "Right now they will be scheming and doing deals too. Every contrada is the same. To the contradas, the Palio is everything. It is more important than life and it is worth dying for. If our own Prior even saw me speaking to that man right now there would be fighting in the streets. That is why you must not tell anyone, Loretta. All this hatred between our contradas – what is it for? We should be one people, united. Instead we squabble and shout taunts at each other like children. We tell the people of the Scallop Shell that they stink of fish, the people of the Eagle that they are yellow cowards and the people of the Porcupine we belittle as fools..." Carlo sighed. "The Palio makes people crazy. When I ride out onto the piazza I must deal with cheats and thugs who try to stop me crossing that finish line. And then, once I am across and I have won the race it is even worse! The crowds surge upon us. The first time it happened I felt like screaming at them to leave us alone. My poor horse! She had just run the race of her life and her reward was to be crushed and terrified by a frenzied mob!"

"If you don't like the Palio," I said with genuine confusion, "then why do you ride in it?"

"Because it is not all like that," Carlo said. "When I line up behind the rope and I wrap my legs tight around Serafina I can feel her heart pounding and I whisper in her ear and she tunes in to my voice instead of the roar of the crowd, then my horse and I are truly one. It is the best feeling in the world to ride a great horse in a race like that, Loretta. I hope you will get to feel it too, someday. But do not think for a moment I do it for fame or for glory or even for our contrada. I do it for the horses. Because I love them."

We were all so proud of Carlo for being chosen as fantino for a third time. Mama and I decided to surprise him.

Piccolina, you have seen the mural of the tree on the stairs and the one of the peacock on my wall. What you haven't yet seen is that there is a third mural, in Carlo's bedroom. It was painted as a gift for him by Mama.

I watched her create this picture, stunned in my admiration of her artistry as she began with an outline in pencil and then worked back over it in oil paints, blending shades of charcoal and silver to capture perfectly the texture of the fur, the steel grey eyes and the curl of the lip above the white fangs, until at last she was finished. Ten times life-size, so large that it covered Carlo's entire wall, she had painted the head of a she-wolf, the Lupa.

Once that was done we set about decorating the whole house in the colours of the contrada – orange and black and white. I even made a costume for our dog, Ludo. It was a black-and-white chequered coat, which I buttoned up along his belly and chest, tying a big orange frill around his neck. The idea was that he was supposed to be a wolf, but Ludo wouldn't cooperate. He kept rolling about and chewing at his outfit trying to get it off. I suppose he must have been hot because he was a shaggy creature. I don't know what breed he was or if he was even a breed at all, probably just a street mutt. He was a dirty-brown colour with floppy ears and this tail, which looked ridiculous because it was too long for his body and it always stuck straight out like a stick.

Mama had prepared a special dinner, but just before Carlo was due to arrive home from the stables she realised we did not have any bread. "Run quickly into town will you, Loretta?" she said. "Grab two loaves for us."

You know the path, Piccolina, for it is the same way I sent you today. Nothing changes in Siena.

I ran the whole way down the avenue of trees and through the Porta Ovile and into the piazza. The usual stalls were set up there in the sunshine, but that day something was different. Standing around the square in small clusters were groups of men – soldiers dressed in black and carrying guns.

"The Blackshirts are all over town," I told my mama when I returned with the bread. "They were running around and yelling with excitement and calling out *Duce!*

Duce! One of them told me I was a good Italian girl getting the bread for my family and he ruffled my hair until it stuck up on end. I think they were drunk!"

"Loretta!" Mama told me off. "You must never speak like that of the Blackshirts. They are the soldiers, the men of *Il Duce*, our great leader."

"Well I don't care – I don't like them," I replied. "Nobody gets to touch my hair and talk to me like I am a child because I am almost twelve."

Carlo loved his mural. And the dinner was delicious. I had helped Mama to cook the meal – stuffed zucchini flowers, and pasta with clams. There was a block of the best chocolate for dessert. I remember it now as one of the happiest nights of my life, when my whole family was still together and we were united and ready for the great battle that was to come very soon, in August, when Carlo would become the hero of our people and win the Palio for a third time. I didn't give another thought to the Blackshirts in the piazza that day. Even if I had, I could never have suspected what was to come.

For over four hundred years, the Palio had been held in the piazza. It had never occurred to anyone that the race would not be run, for nothing in living memory had ever stopped the Palio before. What I didn't realise that day, the first of June, 1940, was that Italy had declared war. The Palio was cancelled and the events that were to follow would change my life for ever.

The Castle of Four Towers

Nonna stopped her story and took a sip from her cup.

"This is very good coffee you have made, Piccolina," she said. "I feel much better now."

"Did they really cancel the Palio?" I asked.

"Yes," Nonna said. "It would have been impossible to run it once war was declared. The whole of Italy was now devoted to the fight and already we felt the pinch of rationing as food became scarce. After a while we found ourselves with barely enough to eat. Bread and pasta were a luxury. Mostly we survived on the vegetables in our garden and the eggs our hens laid. The only meat we had was whatever Carlo managed to hunt in the woods.

Ludo would go with him on his hunting trips and fetch whatever he shot. The poor dog was so thin you could see his ribs sticking out through his shaggy fur. The horses were getting thin too. There was little grass to graze in summer in Siena and so we relied on grain and hay, which we used to buy in. But the war made the prices so crazy we could not afford it any more. We had only enough left in the barn for a few months before we would run out completely. Before Papa went away, he told me what to do when things reached their worst…"

"Your father went away?" I said.

"He had to," Nonna said. "Once Italy declared war, *Il Duce* commanded that all men should join the army. My father was given a uniform and conscripted to the army in Yugoslavia. Mama, Carlo and I went to the station to say goodbye. I had embroidered Papa a handkerchief with his initials and when I presented it to him, he looked enormously sad. I thought maybe he didn't like it, but then I saw that his eyes were welling with tears at saying goodbye to us all. He hugged me tight, and of course by then I was crying too and he wiped away my tears and spoke to me about the horses. 'Look after them, Loretta, for they are the innocents in this and yet they are going to suffer if the war goes on much longer,' he said. 'There will be barely any feed left so ration it carefully and make sure that the mares and foals get the lion's share of anything so they do not grow weak and starve.'

"I told him of course I would care for them. I couldn't bear the idea that our horses would go hungry and I thought if it came to it, I would rather starve myself than watch a mare unable to feed her foal."

Nonna smiled. "My father was clever. He knew how much I loved the horses and I think on the station platform that day he stopped my tears by giving me a job to do, something to think about apart from my own fears. I never heard what he said to Carlo, but I remember that was the only time I saw my brother cry. His cheeks were wet with tears as he saluted my father as he got on the train and Mama threw her arms around Papa while he was in the carriage, hugging him through the window until the train pulled away from the platform…"

Nonna wiped her eyes. "Anyway, that is enough talk of war for one day. It was a long time ago, Lola. We should think of today. I have a special mission for you if you are brave enough. I want you to go back to the red-brick building by the fountain in the Via di Vallerozzi. I want you to take the Prior a letter from me."

Nonna went over to the sideboard in the corner of the kitchen and pulled out a block of writing paper. The pages were creamy and thick and stamped with the crest of the Lupa, a wolf's head against two crossed swords. I watched her handwriting like the tendrils of a vine growing across the page. She was writing in Italian. She finished with her signature and then she folded the paper sharply in three so that it would fit neatly into the envelope and handed it to me.

"There is a letterbox in the front door of the contrada," Nonna said. "Post this through it and come straight home."

I hesitated.

"Nonna?"

"Yes, Piccolina?"

"We didn't just come here for a holiday, did we?"
Nonna looked serious. "No, Piccolina."

"So why did you want to come back?"

Nonna took a deep breath. "I am back for the same reason that I stayed away so long," she said. "Because many years ago, something unforgiveable happened here. And now, perhaps at last, I am ready for forgiveness."

It was near dusk as I walked the streets of the Via di Vallerozzi for the second time that day. *Sure,* I'd said to Nonna. *I'm fine about going back there and posting the letter through the door.* But as I made my way to the red-brick building I had this tight knot growing in my belly. What if the Prior was still there? I had this image in my head of him lunging at me with scissors.

When I reached the contrada I went up to the corner where the streets intersected, where I'd seen the Prior tending the rose bushes. There was no one there. I cast a glance up the street and then turned up the path that led to the entrance.

The front door was really huge, like the door of a

castle, but the mail slot set into it was regular size. I took Nonna's letter and pushed it through. I held the envelope for a moment, hesitating, and my fingers had just let it go when I felt a hand fall down on my shoulder and clasp me from behind.

"Hey!"

I jerked my head around, expecting to see the Prior wielding his scissors.

Instead, I was looking into the face of a boy. He had pale skin and dark eyes, and his black hair was slicked right back off his face so that I could see the hint of a widow's peak at his hairline. It gave him the impression of being older, but I judged he was about my age.

He took one look at me and pulled his hand back as if he had stuck it on a hot plate.

"Hey yourself!" I replied, trying to act sassy to cover up the fact that he had made my heart stop.

"So sorry!" the boy said. "I thought you were someone else."

"Yeah, well, I'm not," I said.

"You speak English?" he asked.

"I speak American," I corrected him.

"I didn't mean to…" the boy stumbled on. "You have your hair tied up and it made you look from behind like you were one of the other boys."

He saw the look on my face. "So sorry again! I keep saying the wrong thing. I didn't mean to be rude. I just…"

"I get what you mean," I smiled. "It's OK."

I stuck out my hand awkwardly – he was standing rather close to me. "My name is Lola, Lola Campione."

"Hello, Lola," he said. "I am Francesco, but everyone calls me Frannie."

I might have boy's hair, I thought, but at least I don't have a girl's name.

Frannie looked behind me. "You were planning to go inside?" he asked.

"Oh no!" I stepped away from the door. "I was just dropping something off. How about you? Are you a member of the Wolf contrada?"

"Me?" Frannie seemed taken aback. "No, I do not belong here. I was delivering the straw bales so that they can prepare the stable for the Palio."

"There's a stable?" I looked the building up and

down. "Where?"

"Downstairs, in the basement." Frannie pointed over the edge of the building to an enclosed courtyard below. "You see those iron bars?"

"They keep horses down there?"

"Not horses," Frannie said. "Just one horse. And not all the time, just for one night – right before the race. Every other night of the year the stall stands empty – the horses do not live here."

"Where do the horses live then?" I asked.

Frannie smiled. "They live with me."

Frannie's grandfather was a horse trainer. He had a stables on the outskirts of the city where he bred, raised and trained horses for the Palio, which he sold to all the contradas. He had almost thirty horses, and right now they were preparing many of them for the race in a month's time.

Frannie told me all of this as we walked down the Via di Vallerozzi together.

"That is so weird," I said. "My dad is a racehorse trainer too, back in New York."

"You like horses?" Frannie seemed pleased.

"Then you should come and visit my farm. Come and see the Palio horses."

"Awesome," I said.

Frannie grinned. "Awesome," he repeated.

"Did I say something funny?" I frowned.

"No, no!" Frannie looked embarrassed. "I like the way you speak… American."

"You speak it pretty good too."

"I have a very good English friend," Frannie said. "He came to ride horses for my grandfather for many years and he taught me how to speak just like him."

We had reached the gates of the Porta Ovile.

"I go this way," he said, pointing in the opposite direction to the avenue of trees that led me home.

"Well, goodbye then, it was nice to meet you," I said.

Frannie dug around in his pocket and found a piece of paper. "I'm going to write down the address of my house. It is just over the hill here, not far. You could walk over tomorrow, if you have time? In the afternoon maybe?"

"Sure," I said.

"OK!" Frannie looked really pleased. He shoved the piece of paper into my hand. I put it in my pocket.

"See you tomorrow then?" he said.

"OK," I replied.

I was just about to walk away when Frannie yelled out to me again. "By the way," he said. "I really like your shoes. They're cool!"

I was wearing those white trainers that Nonna had bought me.

"No, Lola."

Nonna shook her head in disbelief. "No, no, no. You must not get involved with this boy. It is best if we have nothing to do with the people of the Wolf."

"But he's not a Wolf!" I said. "He said he doesn't even belong to the contrada. He was just there to deliver some straw bales."

"Are you certain?"

"Yes!" I said. "He's not a Wolf and he was really nice. And he has horses!"

I couldn't believe she wouldn't let me go! Frannie wanted to be friends with me. Not a single kid in

Ozone Park had ever asked me round to their house.

"Please, Nonna? Please!"

Nonna sighed. "I suppose you can't just sit here with me all day. Very well. What time are they expecting you?"

Frannie had told me to come in the afternoon so I left home at two o'clock. The address he wrote down for me didn't have a street or anything. It just said Castello delle Quattro Torra but he had insisted it would be easy to find.

At Porta Ovile I took the path that I'd seen Frannie take the day before and as soon as I came around the bend of the city walls the Castello delle Quattro Torra was right in front of me set high on the green hills ahead. Frannie was right – you could hardly miss it. A fortress with four turrets, one at each corner, jutting up against the blue sky. The turrets must have been how the place got its name – Castle of the Four Towers.

The castle seemed to dominate the landscape, with deep valleys on either side covered with stands of oak trees. On the hills on the eastern side, instead of the usual olive trees and vineyards, there was bare pasture divided up by post and rail fencing, perfect for horses.

It took me another fifteen minutes on foot to reach the castle. As I got closer, the fortress walls seemed to rise up in front of me. Conifer trees marked out the sweep of the driveway that led to a massive oak front door. It was in proportion to the castle walls and must have been twenty feet high. But there was another normal human-sized entry cut into the door. I turned the heavy cast iron handle and stepped into a cobbled courtyard within the castle walls. I looked up to the sky above and called out.

"Hello?" My voice echoed. "Anybody home?"

I stood and waited but no one came. To my left there was a flight of stairs built into the wall and I went up them and through a doorway. The stairs continued to the next level where there was yet another door, but when I tried this one it was locked. There was a button on the door, I pushed it and heard footsteps on the other side and then the door swung open and there was a dark-haired woman wearing a white dress standing there.

"Lola?"

I stood there for a moment, saying nothing as if I didn't know my own name.

"Yes," I managed to squeak.

The woman smiled at me. "Come in, we've been expecting you." Then, turning back over her shoulder she called out. "Francesco! She is here!"

The woman swung the door open. "Come in," she said. "I am Violetta, Francesco's mother. He won't be long. Make yourself at home."

I was in a living room filled with overstuffed floral couches, antique furniture and vases full of flowers. "This place is amazing!"

"Would you like me to show you around?" Violetta asked.

"She doesn't want to see the castle, Mama," Frannie said as he came bounding in. "She's not a tourist."

"She is new in town, though," Violetta said, "At least I could take her up the turret to see the view."

"Lola didn't come here to look at views," Frannie said. "She came to see horses!"

He grabbed my arm and led me off through the house. "We go this way to the stables," he said.

Through the kitchen and the dining room I followed Frannie. Then through another door and down a narrow staircase and another landing and more stairs until at last we reached an archway that led to the stables. There were twenty crumbling brick loose boxes covered in ivy arranged around a small courtyard. The sound of our footsteps prompted nickers and whinnies from inside the stalls as the horses began to poke their noses out to see what was going on.

"Oh wow!" I breathed.

They were like works of art in a gallery, and the loose boxes, with their split Dutch doors closed at the bottom, but open at the top, served as individual picture frames, capturing each glorious face like it was a portrait as they stuck their long, elegant necks out over the doors.

There was something almost fairy tale about their appearance, as if they weren't real horses at all. The wide set eyes and broad foreheads gave them a fierce intelligence, and the flared nostrils and delicate dish of their muzzles added an exotic quality to their beauty.

"What are they?" I asked.

"You mean their breeding?" Frannie said. "They're Anglo-Arab. Half of their bloodline is pure Thoroughbred like your racehorses, but the other half is Arabian. It's the desert blood that gives them the stamina and the agility they need for the Palio."

"They're beautiful," I said.

Frannie seemed pleased. "My grandfather has a good eye."

Almost every one of the loose-box doors now had a horse looking out over it. There was a pretty dapple grey and a flea-bitten grey right alongside, two bays and a black horse with a thick white stripe down its muzzle.

"How many horses do you have?"

"Twenty in work and some young stock," Frannie said. "Not all of them are ready to race, though. We have maybe ten horses who are good enough to be selected for the Palio."

There was a loud, insistent whinny coming from the stall in the far corner of the yard. The ivy that grew over the stable portico hung low, obscuring my view so that I couldn't see the horse. But I could hear him all right! He was stamping and fretting and kicking up a fuss.

"Is that horse OK?" I asked Frannie.

Frannie frowned. "I moved him there because he was causing too much trouble, always playfighting with the horses in the stalls beside him. But he hates it out of the way in the corner. He likes to be where the action is."

"What do you mean, 'causing trouble'?" I asked.

"Watch," Frannie said. "You'll see."

Beneath the ivy I caught a glimpse of a chestnut muzzle poking over the top of the Dutch door. Then I saw the horse's lips wrap around the bolt on the door and heard the sound of metal scraping.

There was a sudden, heavy clonk as the horse gave the bolt a firm pull and it slid back so that the door unlatched. Then, using his chest, he barged against the bottom door and it swung open and out he strutted into the courtyard. He looked quite pleased with himself as he walked across the cobbles towards us.

"Nico!" Frannie called out to him and the horse

nickered back enthusiastically, lengthening his stride to come to us.

"He opened the door by himself!" I marvelled.

"Yeah," Frannie said darkly. "I thought it was a cute trick too, at first, but I am over it now. He is too smart for his own good, this horse. What is the point of putting him away at night if he decides when he comes and goes?"

He sighed. "At least he hasn't figured out how to open the drawbridge and get out of the courtyard."

The golden chestnut shook his mane as Frannie said this, as if to say "Give me time and I'll figure out how to do that too!"

It was a luxurious mane. Thick and bushy, the colour of honey with streaks of flaxen-blond. The prettiness of the pale colour of his mane was all the more striking against the warm treacle of his chestnut coat.

He stood about sixteen-two, as big as the Thoroughbreds back home, but he was burly, all muscle and sinew, with his rounded hindquarters and crested neck. As he walked up to us he kept shaking his handsome head and nickering as if he was actually having a conversation. I thought he must have been talking to Frannie, but as he got closer he walked straight past him and right up to me, and without any introduction whatsoever he thrust his muzzle into my arms and buried his face in my chest.

"Nico!" Frannie scolded. Then he apologised to me. "I'm sorry. He doesn't usually do that with strangers, it's just he's very affectionate, you know?"

"I can see that!" I giggled.

Nico was butting me with his head, demanding that I scratch his muzzle.

"You are good with him," Frannie observed. "I can tell by the ease that you handle him with, you have grown up around horses."

"Yeah," I said, feeling self-conscious at the compliment, "except I don't think I'd be like this with the horses on our yard!"

"What do you mean?"

"You know, standing around with no halter or anything. Our Thoroughbreds are way too strung out for that. You open the loose-box door and they come out at you like a steam train! They're real high-strung and you have to watch your back. There's one of them, Ginge, he bit a groom a couple of weeks ago, skinned his finger to the bone."

"He sounds very unhappy, this Ginger." Frannie sounded really worried. "Perhaps he needs a hug?"

I gave a hollow laugh. "I don't think anyone is willing to risk getting that close!"

Frannie frowned. "Our horses love company. To be with people is almost a craving in them. It is the Arab blood. Arabians belong to one person only and they are very loyal to their master, like a dog almost."

"Who is Nico's master?" I asked.

"He doesn't have one yet," Frannie said.

"Nobody rides him?"

Frannie laughed. "Oh no, I mean, I do. I ride him. My grandfather broke him in and I am the one that exercises him and does trackwork with him to get him fit and ready to race. But he has no jockey yet for the Palio. One must be chosen."

He looked around the stables. "Many of the horses here belong to different contradas. That grey mare over there? She belongs to the Contrada of the Goose. And that bay, she is the horse of the Snail.

The other one next to her is the horse who will race for the people of the Giraffe."

I looked back at Nico. If I had been clinical about his prospects as a racehorse I would have said that burly physique of his indicated he was built for sprinting, not for distance. But Nonna told me once that a sprinter could win a distance race if he had enough heart. Did Nico have heart? Did he have that all-important will to win? I looked into his eyes, like Nonna had told me, and I saw straight away the softness of him, the quality that made him so affectionate and gentle. I focused hard, trying to see deeper, to find the light, the way Nonna had taught me. Was there that spark that would come alive in him when the race began? A fire that would drive him on and on to the finish line with the raw passion to win at all costs?

There it was! Beneath the gentle, sweet softness of him I caught a glimpse of it. Like catching sight of a wolf dashing through the trees of a forest. I only saw it for a moment, but in that instant I knew it was in him. This horse was special. One day he would be a champion.

"Which contrada will Nico race for?" I asked. And I could feel my heart beating hard as I waited for the answer to come.

"He belongs to the Lupa," Frannie said. "The Contrada of the Wolf."

I headed back to the villa that afternoon with so much news to tell Nonna. Frannie had already asked me to go back again tomorrow

"Come early in the morning," he'd said. "That is when we exercise the horses, before it gets hot. If he is in a good mood I will ask my grandfather if you can ride Nico."

I was so excited about this that if it hadn't been so baking I would have run all the way home. As it was, I was sweating just walking in the afternoon heat.

The key beneath the geranium pot was missing and I was about to knock when the door swung open.

There was a grey-haired man standing in the doorway.

"Hello, Lola," he said.

Lo ti conosco…

I know you

The Prior! In our house!

131

"What are you doing here? Where's my grandmother?"

He didn't answer either of my questions. He gave me this gracious smile, real courteous, as if we were old friends and he always dropped by like this.

"It is a shame I must leave. I would love to stay and visit with you longer," the Prior said, picking up his hat from the hallstand. "But I have a meeting of the contrada to attend…"

I pushed past him into the entrance hall.

"Nonna?" I called out. "Nonna!"

"Calm down. You'll find your grandmother in the kitchen," the Prior said. "Please tell her I will see her soon, Lola." He tipped his hat to me. "It was good to make your acquaintance again."

He shut the door behind him and I ran, my heart pounding.

"Nonna? Nonna! Are you OK?"

"I am fine, Piccolina." My grandmother was sitting at the kitchen table.

"What was he here for?"

"Because I asked him to come, Piccolina," Nonna said. "I wanted to talk to him."

"About what?" I asked.

Nonna didn't answer at first. Then she said, "There is still much about my past that you do not yet understand, Piccolina. I told you the first part of my story yesterday, and now my conversation with the Prior has awakened many memories. Please, come sit with me. I have much more to tell you…"

Blackshirts

At school every morning the teachers would make us listen to the radio broadcast. The news stories were very exciting, telling us about how marvellously Italy was doing in the war. Our fearless soldiers were winning every battle. At the end of the broadcast we would stand up behind our desks and the teacher would ask us: "To whom victory?"

"To us! To us!" we would chorus, giving the fascist salute.

I didn't know that it was all a lie, that the Italian army was losing horribly and thousands of men were dying. My father was in terrible danger, risking his life every day on the battle lines. *Il Duce*, the man that my mama loved as a great leader, was not a good man. He was on the same side as Hitler and the Nazis, and his cruel fascists, the Blackshirts, were brutal to their own people in order to keep us under their control.

I heard whispers on the school playground about the things the Blackshirts would do to you if they decided you were a traitor.

"They make you drink castor oil," Marco told me.

"Ewww! Why would they do that?"

"It makes your tummy sick so you poo in your pants and then they beat you with their sticks," Marco insisted.

"You're making it up!" I told him.

"It's true," Marco insisted. "Sometimes they beat you so hard you die."

Marco was my best friend. We had shared a bond from the very first week at school when he found me crying in the playground because one of the big boys had stolen my lunch.

"Don't let them see you cry," he'd told me firmly as he gave me his handkerchief to dry my eyes. Then he'd sat down on the wall and shared his own bread and cheese with me, telling me jokes while I was eating so that I nearly choked because I was laughing so hard.

Marco had an outrageous sense of humour. That was

why I didn't believe him at first about the castor oil, even though it was true, because it sounded like the sort of thing he would make up. He wore too-big shorts that made his rail-thin legs look like two sticks and he had moon-pale skin, black eyes and jet-black hair that always fell over his face though he tried to slick it back. From the day he shared his lunch with me, we were inseparable, always talking and laughing and telling secrets to each other. But the biggest secret we shared was our friendship.

One day, not long after we'd met, I took Marco home after school to play at my house. My mama opened the door to us, took one look at Marco and her face went taut in a thin-lipped scowl. She did not open the door to let him in.

"Go home, boy," she told Marco stiffly. "You can't be here. Loretta has forgotten that she has family commitments." She ushered me roughly inside and then slammed the door in his face.

"But, Mama," I protested. "I wanted to play –"

"What were you doing bringing that boy home?" Her voice was full of anger like I had never heard it before. "You know he is a Porcupine! He cannot be allowed into our house!"

I burst into tears – remember, Piccolina, I was only six years old when this happened.

"But, Mama," I blubbed. "Please! I want to play with him!"

"Loretta!" Mama was stony-faced. "His family are no good. They are nothing but miserable liars and stinking thieves."

"Marco isn't a liar."

"Do not defend him!" Mama snapped. "The Porcupines have nothing but hatred for us. For hundreds of years they have been our enemies. You must not have anything more to do with him."

"But he's my best friend!" My sobs had become little hiccups.

"Loretta." Mama shook her head. "Stop crying. I do this for the best. You will have many friends, boys and girls. But they will all be Wolf cubs just like you. And you will marry a Wolf too. This Marco, he is nothing. You must never talk to him again."

Marco was not allowed in my house. Not only that, Mama said if he even dared to enter the district of the Via di Vallerozzi he would be beaten up by the local Wolf boys.

At school the next day, I tried to do what Mama told me.

I would not look at Marco in the classroom. At lunchtime I hid in the branches of a big oak tree, but he climbed up and found me. He looked even paler than usual, his black eyes sunken, and I knew he'd been crying.

"My mama says I have to stay away from you," I told him.

"Mine too," he said.

We sat there in the tree for a while, then Marco said to me.

"I won't tell them if you don't."

Both of us knew at that moment how serious the secret was that we were keeping. If our teachers or the other kids saw us together they might have told their parents or reported us to the contradas. We never spoke to each other in class or acknowledged each other in front of the other children. Instead we developed a secret sign language, drawing symbols in the air with our fingers to each other, communicating in code across the classroom.

If I traced out a circle and a V that meant we should meet beside the drinking fountain next to the library. A wiggle of the fingers and a clenched fist from Marco meant I should wait for him at lunchtime in the grove of trees beside the bicycle racks.

Even at these hidden meeting places it was impossible to really speak to each other without fear of getting caught. The only place we were really safe was what Marco referred to as "neutral territory" – an old abandoned villa, high in the hills to the southern side of the city.

We rode there on our horses – it was too far to go on foot. Marco was an excellent rider and I was certain he would become a fantino for the Porcupines one day. When we first met he had this little brown pony called Piccolo. Then later, when he was about nine, he was given Clara, a grey mare with dark dapples. She was a tricky horse with a hot nature, but Marco was a kind rider and he handled her gently so they suited each other.

We couldn't ride together, of course. Usually I rode the paths alone, but sometimes Carlo would go with me. My brother was the only one who knew about Marco. He did not mind at all that my best friend was a Porcupine. Carlo did not care about the contradas, as I have said before. All he cared about was the horses.

Carlo was with me on the ride to the villa the day that I earnt my nickname.

By now my father had been gone for almost a year. The war was going very badly for Italy and despite the best efforts of *Il Duce* to keep up the appearance that we were winning, there were murmurs of unrest. In the city everyone still greeted the Blackshirts with the customary salute, but behind closed doors people were anxious and afraid.

"They give people castor oil," I said to Carlo, repeating what Marco had told me. "They stick a funnel in your mouth and make you drink it."

I was riding Stella as always and Carlo was on Serafina. It was a sunny day and we were letting the horses walk freely, reins loose as we talked.

Carlo had been very quiet for the whole ride. When I told him about the castor oil, he looked really upset and then he said, "I have to tell you something. About what happened yesterday when Mama sent me to Signor Garo's store to get bread."

"You told us the store was closed," I said.

"It wasn't closed," Carlo replied. "When I got to town there were Blackshirts everywhere, like there always are. They were marching about as if they owned the place and then I saw a large group of them armed with sticks. They went into Signor Garo's store. Before I could get there I heard shrieks and shouting coming from inside and then suddenly there was this crash and broken glass flying everywhere. The next thing I knew Signor Garo was lying in the street covered in his own blood. They had thrown him through the plate-glass window!"

"But why Signor Garo?" I said. "Why hurt him, of all people?"

"He is a Jew," my brother said. "And the Nazis hate the Jews so now we Italians hate them too."

"Poor Signor Garo!"

Carlo looked pained. "I should have helped him, Loretta. After all he has done for us, and instead I just let him get beaten up right there in the street." He wiped his eyes angrily. "I wanted to help him, but I did not dare. No one did. We just left him there, lying in his own blood while the Blackshirts took whatever they wanted from the store."

I felt terrible for Signor Garo. He was a very kind man. With my father away fighting he had let Mama run up a huge bill, buying flour and other items on credit.

I was silent for a moment considering this. Then I asked, "What happened to him?"

"They took him away," Carlo said. "Anyone who disagrees with the Blackshirts gets taken away. There is talk of torture, and beatings. No one who is taken by the

Blackshirts comes back again."

"Without him, we will starve."

"We will be all right," Carlo muttered. "I can hunt for meat. We have the garden. We'll manage..."

As Carlo said this, we rounded the corner and there right in front of us was a checkpoint. Two army jeeps had been parked across the road, back to back with a narrow gap between them, just big enough for a car to drive through. This gap was barred by a wooden pole, creating a makeshift barrier balanced between the flatbeds of the jeeps. The three Blackshirts who had created this road block were laughing and smoking, playing cards on the bonnet of one of the vehicles.

"What's this for?" I whispered to Carlo.

"They make the cars stop," Carlo said. "They check them, supposedly looking for traitors and spies, but really they just steal whatever they want and then move the pole to let you pass."

Looking back, the smart thing to do at that moment would have been to ride up to the Blackshirts and calmly allow them to inspect our bags and the horses. After all, we were Italians, not foreigners, and the only thing we had on us was a precious bar of chocolate, saved for many months, which I was planning to share with Marco when we reached the villa. But I didn't want to give them my chocolate. Also, I was so scared by the stories Carlo had been telling me that at that moment, when I saw the men with their guns, I panicked. Perhaps they might get suspicious about what we were doing and what if they started to question us? If they discovered our hideaway and Marco was already there then they would tell the contrada and I wouldn't be able to see him any more.

"We're not stopping," I whispered to Carlo.

"What are you talking about, Loretta?" Carlo hissed back. "Of course we're stopping!"

"Shorten your reins," I warned him through gritted teeth, "and get ready to go!"

"Loretta! No, you can't be serious..." Carlo tried to argue with me but when he saw the look of resolve on my face he knew it was pointless.

"You're crazy, you know that?" he muttered. Then, cursing my name under his breath, he kicked Serafina on. With a swift tap of my heels and a cluck of my tongue I urged Stella into a gallop too and fell into stride right behind Carlo.

Ahead of us, the soldiers, who had been absorbed in

their card game, suddenly realised what was going on. We were galloping towards them and we clearly had no intention of pulling up our horses.

"Hey!" one of them cried. "No! Stop!"

He began to fumble around on his back for his rifle and I felt sick at the sight of him reaching for the gun, but it was too late to change my mind now. Ahead of me, Carlo was in full gallop.

One of the Blackshirts waggled his gun at Carlo, but the others obviously thought the whole situation was amusing. One of them stepped away from the jeeps and began to wave his hands up and down indicating for us to slow down. His face changed, however, when he saw that Carlo wasn't stopping. Now he too reached for his rifle, shouting out to the third man, gesturing at him to move quickly.

I watched Serafina as she hesitated for a moment, but she was a good Palio horse and the shouting and commotion did not faze her. She saw the barricade, and her ears pricked forward as she recognised the checkpoint rail for what it was to her – a brightly painted showjump fence.

At just the right moment Carlo called out "Hup" and

Serafina took one last stride and then lifted up in the air, taking the rail for all the world as if she were a grand prix jumper. She gave such an almighty stag leap that I saw Carlo clutch a handful of her mane to keep from sliding off, but he had the natural balance of a Palio rider and he quickly righted himself, driving her on.

Stella and I were only a few strides behind him, but in this brief time the Blackshirts had finally gathered their wits. They moved in unison to block our path, standing side-by-side in front of the checkpoint rail. Two of them had their guns pointed straight at me. On the other side of the blockade I could see my brother pull up Serafina and look back at me in despair. He was shaking his head at me as if to say, "give up". There was no way I could jump the rail now.

Later on, Carlo and Marco would make a big fuss about my courage that day. But I swear it wasn't bravery that drove me to do what I did. It was pure instinct. We were moving too fast to pull up, and besides, I trusted Stella. I knew she would not fail me. So when the men closed ranks in front of that rail I did not even think to stop. Instead, I trained my eyes on the jeep to the right of me and took a deep breath and rode on.

That's right, I told Stella, closing my legs hard against her sides. We're going over it.

I had jumped small things before that. A fallen log once or twice, and low fences in the fields near our house, but I had never jumped anything the size of a jeep! If you'd asked me to jump it again in cold blood I don't think I could have done it, but the adrenaline was coursing through my veins and I could feel Stella gathering herself up, and I knew that she could make it.

The jeep was so wide that as we hung in mid-air I worried for a moment that she wouldn't make the spread, but of course she cleared it easily. We landed neatly too, and then Stella surged forward once more, and by the time the Blackshirts had pulled themselves together, leapt into the jeep and started to drive after us, Carlo and I had already made our escape, heading off the main road and diverting along the narrow paths in the woods that led us to the villa where Marco was waiting for us.

Marco didn't believe the story at first. He thought we were making it up – but then he saw the state our horses were in, sweating and blowing, and the way we kept checking anxiously out of the windows in case the Blackshirts had followed us, and then he knew it was true and he told me I was a hero.

"A hero?" Carlo was stunned. "We are lucky we didn't get shot!"

He smiled at me. "My sister, *Loretta Scavezzecolla*!"

It means Daredevil.

And that is how I got my name.

Romeo, Juliet and Me

I set my alarm before I went to bed that evening. Frannie had said come early to exercise the horses, so I figured four a.m. would be OK.

I woke up before it even rang, like I usually do. I didn't want my bedroom light to disturb Nonna. She knew I was going to Frannie's, and there was no need to wake her, so I went about finding my things in the dark, fumbling around and working by feel. I was pretty much used to getting dressed this way after sharing a room with Donna back home. She hated it if I woke her up when I was getting ready to go to the track. Donna never got up early. "I need beauty sleep," she would groan.

She could sleep for a hundred years and it wouldn't help.

After sharing a room with Donna all my life, putting up with her constant blibber blabber about whichever boy she was dating, I loved having my own room at last. Only I kind of missed having Johnny and Vincent around. My brothers argued a lot, mostly about dumb stuff, never about anything important. You could hear them when they were riding track, bickering their way around the course, galloping side-by-side so they could shout back and forth. Afterwards, they'd cool their horses off before taking them to the wash bay. Four workouts apiece and they'd be done, heading over to the bodega, both ordering the same thing from Sherry, the breakfast tortilla with extra bacon on the side.

"The same old routine, baby sis," Vincent had told me on the phone when Nonna and I had called home. I could hear Johnny in the background shouting something and trying to grab the phone off him, and it was hearing them fighting that made me miss them.

Then Dad took the phone off both of them. He

wanted to speak to Nonna first. I could hear her running through checklists with him.

"Get Johnny to breeze Ginge tomorrow then blow him out before the race this weekend," she said. Then a pause as she listened to Dad and I saw her shake her head. "Uh-uh, he needs protein. You should add a scoop of Hanley Formula to his feed, Ray. That horse has to put on some fast muscle if he's going to be ready to race in the fall…" Then, once all the horses had been dealt with, the phone got passed back again to me.

"Lola?"

"Hi, Dad."

"You sound like you're just down the road. Good reception, huh?"

"Clear as a bell."

"How's the old country?"

"Pretty old, all right."

We continued talking like that about nothing much. I described the villa to him, told him about the fresh bread at the markets and the sunny weather. I didn't say anything about being chased by the Prior or about meeting Frannie. If Dad knew I was going riding on some stranger's racehorse he would have had said no way.

I had packed my jodhpurs when I left New York. Not really because I'd been expecting that I would get to ride, but because they were my comfy pants. Back home I wore them around the house all the time, which made Donna go on about how I needed a wardrobe makeover. Like she would know fashion, with her tiny shorts and high heels.

I dressed in my jods now, with sneakers and a light cotton blouse. I tied a sweatshirt that said *New York State* around my waist because there was a chill to the air and I thought I might get cold walking to the castle.

As it was, I never undid the sweatshirt. By the time I got to the castle gates the sun had broken the horizon and was beginning to seep over the fields, warming them with a soft tangerine glow. Through the door-within-a-door I entered the courtyard, footsteps echoing on the cobbles, and walked up the stairs. I rang the front door buzzer and waited, but no one answered. I rang again. Perhaps Frannie was already at the stables and I was too late…

"Coming! Coming! Wait!" I heard a voice and the patter of someone scurrying barefoot across the floor, and then the door swung open and there was Violetta in her dressing gown, hair tied up in a messy topknot.

"Lola!" She looked worried. "Is everything OK? What's wrong?"

"Umm." I was confused. "I'm fine. Is Frannie down at the stables?"

"Francesco?" Violetta rubbed her eyes, she seemed baffled by the question. "No, he is in bed, asleep."

"Oh." I was taken aback. I realised now that she had been in bed too. I had woken her up.

"Frannie told me to come early to ride the horses…"

"But this is not early. It is the middle of the night!" Violetta exclaimed.

"I… I'm so sorry…" I stammered. "I thought… I should go…"

"No," Violetta said, regaining her good humour. "Come in, please. I will wake Frannie."

I stood in the middle of the living room feeling

wildly uncomfortable. A few moments later Violetta came back. "He is getting dressed," she said. "He will not be long. Meanwhile, let me give you that tour I promised."

Violetta's tour started the same way Frannie and I had gone yesterday, through the kitchen and dining room, but instead of going downstairs towards the stables, we stayed on the same level and headed towards the turret at the rear of the castle. I was beginning to understand the layout now. The castle was like a house with a hole in the middle. All the rooms were built around the outside of the great courtyard, with the main living space wrapping all the way around on the second floor and then four staircases at each corner of the castle, each one leading up to a turret. The turrets at the back of the castle were only small, like the sort where princesses in fairy tales are trapped waiting for their princes. But the front two turrets were larger and they contained bedrooms and bathrooms – the "family rooms" as Violetta called them.

Violetta was quite serious when she said she was giving me a tour. She spoke about the castle like one of those professional museum guides as we went from room to room. "Built in 1302, it has featured in many paintings over the years. It was an important fortress during the Siena War in 1555…"

I was half-listening. History didn't interest me much when it was all about years and wars. The walls of the castle were all raw brick, some of them hung with tapestries and art. I followed Violetta, smiling and nodding politely. We had almost completed the circuit and we were walking down the long corridor that led us back to the front of the castle when I saw the painting. It was draped on either side with red velvet curtains, like those famous paintings in art galleries. The curtains were tied back with gold rope with tassels on the ends. The painting was as tall as me and twice as wide, so that when you stood in front of it you felt as if you could climb into the picture and join the couple who were standing there. I recognised them immediately, the girl on the balcony with the boy gazing up at her. His hand on his heart, her arm outstretched to him, imploring him to scale the walls to reach her.

"You know this picture?" Violetta asked.

I nodded. "It's Romeo and Juliet, right?"

She smiled. "The two star-crossed lovers of Shakespeare. But this work was painted a hundred years before he wrote his play. Look more closely and tell me what else you see."

What else? I stared hard at the painting. And then I saw the colours flash – the black and white harlequin print sleeves and the brilliant orange bodice of Juliet's gown. And glowing on her milky white outstretched hand, an ornate gold ring with green emerald eyes, in the shape of a wolf's head.

"She's a Lupa," I said.

"Quite right." Violetta was impressed. "And look at the boy. He wears black and blue, burgundy and white. The colours of the Istrice – the Porcupine contrada."

She lifted up her hand to the painting as if she longed to touch it, but she held back. "The painting is called *Mariotto and Gianozza*. It is based on the story of a boy and a girl who are madly in love, but cannot be together because they are from different contradas. In the end, they both die of their love for each other. It is a very sad story, very similar to the one that Shakespeare would write over a century later. Shakespeare set his play in Verona, but historians say that the true birthplace of the story of *Romeo and Juliet* was right here in Siena."

I gazed at the painting. "It's beautiful. Have your family owned it a long time?"

"No." Violetta shook her head. "My father bought it at an auction. He had to sell many of his best Palio horses to afford it, and I never understood quite why it meant so much to him to have it. I mean, I love it too, but for him it is more than that. Sometimes, late at night I will find him here, just staring at it, as if he is a million miles away."

She smiled at me. "Come on, Frannie will be dressed by now. Let's have some breakfast."

Breakfast was a cappuccino and a platter of tiny hot panini, little bread rolls, with fresh jam. There was yoghurt too, with hazelnuts and a bowl of fresh raspberries to spoon on top.

Frannie arrived from his bedroom upstairs in one of the turrets as Violetta was laying breakfast out on the table. He looked half-asleep, with his long dark hair still tousled and the buttons of his shirt done up in the wrong holes.

"I'm sorry," I told him. "Back home we ride the first horses at four-thirty. I thought when you said early you meant, you know, early."

"It's my fault," Frannie said, fixing the shirt buttons. "I didn't say a time. Anyway, it's good to get up with the sunrise for once."

Violetta laughed at this. "That's not what you said when I came to wake you up!"

Frannie groaned. "I'm not a morning person, OK?"

"Well," Violetta said. "It's now almost six. The others will be here in an hour."

She had put one of the bread rolls and a pot of coffee on a tray. "I'd better take your grandfather his breakfast."

"OK." Frannie pushed his chair back and stood up. "Lola and I will go ahead and get the horses ready."

"Can I be the one to groom Nico?" I couldn't hold back any longer from asking. In bed last night I'd been unable to sleep for thinking about him. I lay there and marvelled at the fine smoothness of his coat, and the long, slender legs and the power of his haunches and muscular, arched neck. All traits of the Arabian – proof that long ago his forebears had galloped the desert sands.

Those Arabians, chosen for their stamina and heart, had been crossbred with the leggy, elegant Italian Thoroughbred. Their bloodlines intermingled over centuries of breeding to create Nico. But it was not blood alone that made him special. Nico possessed a brilliance that belonged to him alone. It was there when I looked into his liquid brown eyes that first time. Straight away then I knew that here was a horse who would dig deep at the crucial moment and try for you until his heart broke in two. We had only been together briefly, but already I was so sure that I was right about this horse. I knew Nico was a champion.

"Sure," Frannie said as he led me down the stairs to the stables. "You can take care of Nico."

We came out through the stairwell into the light of the stableyard and there was Nico. Frannie had moved him back to his favourite old stall right in the middle of the row and he had his head over the door waiting for us. Immediately he took up nickering like he had last time, and at the sight of me alongside Frannie I swear his eyes brightened. He gave his mane a vigorous shake and let out a full-throated whinny.

Wow, I thought. Even more handsome than I remembered.

"You'd better go to him before he takes matters into his own hands and opens the loose box door again," Frannie said.

"Where's his halter?" I asked.

"There's one in the stall, but you won't need it," Frannie said. "He'll stand still for you while you brush him."

It seemed like a shame to put a halter on a face as beautiful as Nico's. I was mesmerised by the exquisiteness of him. The way that white star on his forehead extended into a slender blaze that trickled down the centre of his face and tapered off at the muzzle. How his ears, which were small and dainty, curved inwards in an arc so that the points of them almost touched. That must have been an Arabian thing because I'd never seen a Thoroughbred with ears like that. I loved his dished face and wide nostrils – that was something Nonna always said to look for. "A big nostril is good! They can't breathe through their mouths like we do when we run, Lola. When they gallop the nostrils widen like trumpets to get as much air as they can."

Nonna didn't just show me how to look a horse in the eye to see greatness. She also taught me practical stuff like the nostrils. She had the most critical eye in the world when it came to examining a horse's conformation. Every time a new Thoroughbred came onto our yard she would give it the once-over and say to me, "Tell me what's wrong with this one, Lola."

Sometimes I'd find an obvious flaw, like a ewe neck or parrot mouth, and then Nonna would take over and she'd show me how to hunt out every hidden weakness. Sickle hocks and upright pasterns, a splint or long cannon bones, a high wither or a roach back. With each horse I learnt to seek out the fault that might hold them back from being a winner or cause them to break down mid-race.

Yesterday I had been blinded by the glory of Nico, but today as I let myself into his stall, I tried to put my emotions aside and be bloodless in my appraisal. I checked him thoroughly for all the signs of a horse that is built to run, looking at the broadness of his chest, the thickness of his bone, the angle of the shoulder and the way the neck was set onto it. I went through every detail like Nonna had shown me, but I couldn't find anything wrong. In every sense this horse was perfect.

The hooves were the last thing I checked. I picked them up one at a time to examine the soles. "Good boy, Nico," I murmured. "Give me your hind leg now…" I bent down by his hindquarters, grasping the left leg and raising it to my knee. I was crouched over like that when I heard someone say, "You must be Lola."

I put Nico's hoof down and stood up.

The old man leaning over the stable door had the lean body of a jockey, and even with his wrinkles and grey hair he instantly reminded me of Frannie. They shared the same dark eyes and widow's peak hairline.

"I am Signor Fratelli. Nice to meet you."

He stuck his hand over the stable door for me to shake.

"Nice to meet you, sir."

"Frannie says you are from America?"

"That's right," I said. "New York."

"And why are you here?"

"Umm." I was taken aback. "Frannie said if I wanted, I could ride…"

"No, no," Signor Fratelli shook his head. "Not here at the stables. I ask why are you in Siena?"

"Oh!" I got what he meant. "I came with my grandmother. She grew up here. We're on holiday."

"And what is the name of your grandmother?" he asked.

"Loretta Campione," I said. "Well, that's her married name. But when she lived here it would have been Loretta Alessi, I guess."

I saw a strange look pass across his face. Or was I imagining it? Anyway he didn't say anything else about it.

"You know how to ride, Lola?" he asked.

"Yes, sir," I said. "We have racehorses back home."

Signor Fratelli nodded his head at Nico.

"You like this horse?" he asked.

"He's amazing," I said.

"He is the best horse in our stable," Signor Fratelli said. "You have a good eye, I think."

Then he handed me the bridle from the hook outside the stall.

"You will ride him today."

"OK," I said. "Thank you."

My heart was hammering at my chest. Signor Fratelli gave another grunt to confirm that all was good and then began to shuffle off.

"Excuse me, Signor Fratelli, sir?"

"Yes, Lola?"

"Where is his saddle?"

Signor Fratelli shook his head. "No saddles, you ride bareback. He is a Palio horse, that is the way we do it here. You can do that, yes?"

"Yes, Signor Fratelli." I felt foolish all of a sudden, like I'd just asked for training wheels for my racing bike.

In the stall I buckled up Nico's bridle. I was wrong. That face looked even prettier with the dark brown leather defining it. When I led him out into the yard Signor Fratelli was there with Frannie and three others. Two boys and a girl. The girl had honey-blonde hair, I figured she was only around fifteen or sixteen but she was quite tall. The boys were shorter than her, and they seemed to be about the same age as Johnny and Vincent. They had jet-black curls and blue eyes and looked so alike I guessed they must be twins.

"Lola," Frannie said, "This is Antonia, Umberto and Leonardo.

"*Ciao, Lola!*" Antonia said without much conviction.

"*Ciao,*" Umberto deadpanned.

Leonardo didn't even bother with a hello. He just hung his head and acted like I wasn't even there.

"Hi." I summoned up a smile. I was wondering why all of them were here and where were the fantinos?

"Shall we go then?" Antonia asked, looking at her watch as if time was being wasted.

"You're riding with us?" I asked.

Frannie laughed. "Yes. Antonia, Umberto and Leonardo are the jockeys who work our horses."

"You race in the Palio?"

"I don't." Antonia frowned. "I just exercise the horses. Racing is not my thing. But these two…" She gestured at the twins. "They are hopefuls."

"We are in training," Umberto clarified. "We ride for Signor Fratelli and for a few of the other stables in Siena."

"The good ones only," Leonardo said, "with the fast horses. We like to win."

"Frannie says you race horses back home in America?" Antonia said this as if she clearly didn't believe a word of it. "They let kids ride there?"

"My dad is a trainer and I ride sometimes. Not in actual races…"

Antonia turned her back on me mid-sentence and vaulted up lightly onto the back of her bay mare as deftly as a circus gymnast.

"So you can ride?" she said. "Well, let's hope you can keep up then."

I saw her cast a sideways glance at Umberto who

smirked at this. Leonardo had vaulted up onto his horse, and now Umberto mounted too.

"You want a leg-up?" Frannie was at my side. He cupped his hands and took my knee and thrust me up in the air and onto Nico.

Then he vaulted up onto his horse just like the others had done.

Antonia had been gabbling away to the others in Italian, but as soon as Frannie was onboard she stopped talking and took up the slack in her reins. "Everyone OK then?"

Before I could reply she had urged her horse forward into a trot and then straight into a canter, clattering across the cobblestones of the stableyard. Leonardo gave a whoop and fell in behind her and Umberto and Frannie both kicked their horses on too. I only just had time to clutch at my own reins before Nico, terrified at being left behind, surged forward like a racehorse breaking from the gate.

Had Antonia gone before I was ready on purpose to unseat me? She was already out through the archway of the castle wall. Here the cobblestones ended and the dirt road began, soft sandy loam almost like a racetrack. Antonia let her mare find her footing and then clucked her on into a fast gallop. I'd seen jockeys breeze their horses this fast back home at Aqueduct, but that was on the flat terrain of a racetrack. Antonia was riding downhill on a sharply twisting road that snaked back and forth in loops down the slopes of the olive grove, descending into the valley of giant oak trees below.

I had no choice but to keep pace with her and the others, even though I felt myself slipping forward, having to grip for all I was worth with my thighs to keep my balance and stay on bareback. With each turn I felt gravity threatening to swoop Nico out from underneath me.

I could have fallen off on the first turn for all Antonia would have known. She never once looked back to see if I was OK. She set a blistering pace galloping down along the twisting pathway into the valley. When we reached the oak grove we were riding on flat ground once more and I could stop worrying so much about staying onboard and begin to focus on the pack ahead of me. Antonia was still in the lead and the others had fallen into formation behind her, the twins riding side-by-side, followed by Frannie and then me.

Beneath me, Nico was galloping hard, his breath coming in excited snorts. So far he had run purely of his own accord, mostly driven by the urge that horses have to remain at all costs with the herd. But I hadn't asked him for anything yet. And now, as the path flattened out ahead of us and Antonia's bay mare begin to flag a little, Leonardo and Umberto split apart and slowed their horses and I saw the gap open up.

"Now, Nico!" I wrapped my legs around him, no longer using them to cling on, but to signal to him that the race was on, we were making our move.

Instantly I felt him surge, his stride opening up, his legs working like pistons beneath us. As the others faded he was rising to the challenge, and I realised now that he had been hating it all this time down the hill as I'd held him back with all my strength because he couldn't bear to be at the rear. With every fibre of his being he wanted to be out front and that was where we were going now, swallowing the ground with every stride, passing Frannie and then

Leonardo and then Umberto until at last there was only Antonia ahead of us. If she hadn't bothered to look back at me before, she was certainly taking a good look over her shoulder now. Riding like a track jockey she manoeuvred her mare to block me.

She had me jammed behind her horse's rump as we came out of the woods and into the sunlight, up the other side of the valley. I had to hand it to her, she rode like a pro, never letting a gap open. I was looking for a space, but I couldn't get past. Furious at being held back, Nico was fighting me, attempting to reef the reins from my fingers, but there was nowhere to go.

"Easy, Nico." I kept my grip, but I knew I couldn't control him like this much longer. If we couldn't get past Antonia by sneaking through, our only option was to pull out and run wide. We would need to go further and faster to take the lead, but if Nico had the power and speed that I suspected he possessed, then we could make it.

"OK then, you want to run? Let's see what you've got!"

Nico gave a snort of indignation as I yanked

the rein hard to the left, but then he saw the track opening up and he understood me. He flattened out his stride and when I drove him on he thrust forward with such speed he left me breathless. I had never felt a horse move so fast before. The way he stretched out so that within just a few short strides we were alongside Antonia. I saw the shocked expression on her face as she looked across at me, and then we were gone, taking the lead and moving further in front, until we were a good five lengths ahead of Antonia and more than ten ahead of the others.

I think he could have run for ever that day, but when we crested the hill and I realised that this must be where we finished, he pulled up real obedient, softening instantly to my touch and coming back easily. I think he knew the race was over, and he had nothing more to prove because he slowed to a canter, giving little happy snorts, and then to a trot and a walk, his sides heaving, his neck and flanks frothing with sweat.

I turned around to look behind me at the others and the first thing I saw was Antonia with this smile like sunshine on her face. And the others too all whooping and calling out to each other in Italian, and then Antonia was right beside me and she had flung an arm over my shoulder, laughing as if we were old friends.

And then, with a wave to Frannie who was the last to join us, she called out. "Frannie! You win."

"But he came last." I was confused.

"Not the race," Leonardo said, pulling up his horse next to me and smiling. "Our bet. We had a bet with Frannie, he said you could ride, but we didn't believe him. And now we do."

Frannie rode up alongside us. "I told you, didn't I?" he taunted the others. "Happy now?"

"Yeah," Umberto said, giving me a pat on the back. "The kid's OK, she can ride with us anytime."

Frannie looked pleased as he rode up alongside me. "I knew you wouldn't let me down," he said proudly. "Brava. Brava, *Lola Scavezzecolla.*"

Into the Woods

Scavezzecolla. That is what Marco and Carlo both called me after that day when I jumped the roadblock. What they did not realise was that afterwards I would lie awake at night, petrified that the Blackshirts had recognised me and they were going to turn up suddenly and rip me out of bed and take me away and torture me with castor oil for making them look so stupid.

There was a change in Mama's tone now when she spoke about the Blackshirts. She had once admired them as good men. Now, after what happened to Signor Garo, I knew she thought differently. Our town had always been full of rivalries and distrust between the contradas. Now an uglier division had silently begun to consume us. The rich and the privileged, living in luxury despite the war, continued to support *Il Duce* and his fascists. The rest of us, poor and starving for the most part, secretly began to suspect that something was very wrong. At school, as we gave our salutes and stood to attention and chanted about victory, I started to wonder whether we were being told the whole truth. There were rumours flying around that perhaps we were not so victorious after all. If we were winning the war then why were the Blackshirts beating up anyone who disagreed with them?

By the summer of 1943 the Palio had already been cancelled two years in a row, and it seemed that it would be cancelled a third time with no end to the war in sight. Carlo was very upset about this, he wanted so desperately to race Serafina, but the war had interrupted his plans and the bay mare was now almost nine, too old for the demands and dangers of the racetrack. And so Carlo turned his attention instead to Stella, and began to train her in the hope that by the time the Palio was run again she would be ready.

"She will be a better horse even than Serafina," Carlo insisted. "She has the speed to win, plus she is surefooted enough to take the corners and fearless enough to face up to the body slams and beatings that we will take out there in the piazza."

By now my father had been gone for two years and Carlo, who was almost eighteen, knew that if the war did not finish soon he would not be joining the fantinos on the racetrack, but instead would be forced to enlist in the fascist army.

My brother was not a coward. He was very brave. "But to join the fascists is the same thing as fighting on the side of the Nazis," he told me, "and I will not fight for Hitler."

It was July and we were hoping against the odds that an announcement would be made that the Palio would be held again in August. Instead, there was much more dramatic news.

"*Il Duce* has been thrown out!" My brother raced through the front door of our house, panting and puce-faced. He had run home all the way from the piazza. "There are celebrations. It is the fall of the fascists!"

The joy came too soon. It was true, *Il Duce* was gone, taken off to prison. But the war continued and it became more dangerous than ever to stand up to the Blackshirts, because the Nazis were in Italy too and the Blackshirts had joined forces with them.

"We need to rise up against them," Carlo announced. "My friends, Gino and Vincenzo and Arturo, you know them, they are all ready to join the fight for freedom."

"You are just boys!" Mama told him.

"Together we will become an army," Carlo insisted. "Not all of the rich and powerful in this town are fascists. The Prior and the Capitano of the Contrada of the Wolf are both good men. We can trust them to help us."

"If the Blackshirts discover that you are on the side of the freedom fighters they will come for you," Mama said. "They will interrogate and torture you until you tell them everything and then hang you as traitors."

"You are right, Mama," Carlo agreed. "And that is why I must go."

"Go?" Mama said. "But where? You cannot be safe anywhere in Siena."

"To the woods," Carlo said. "We'll set up camp, wait for others to join the cause, and plan our next move."

"When will you go?" Mama asked.

"Tonight," Carlo said. I saw that his eyes were alight with excitement in a way that had been missing ever since they stopped running the Palio.

That night I sat on the end of my brother's bed and

watched as he packed his bag. He didn't take much with him, just some warm clothes and a sleeping roll.

"When will you come back?" I asked.

"Very soon, Loretta," Carlo said. "You will see. Now that *Il Duce* has gone, Italy has woken up. More and more of us will turn against the Nazis and we will become an army and return to fight for our people."

"Can't I come with you? I wouldn't be any trouble. I'll do whatever you say."

Carlo looked up from his packing and saw the tears welling in my eyes. He put down the bag and wrapped his arms around me in a tight bear hug.

"Who would look after the horses if you came?" he said. "You have a job to do here, Loretta. Do you know how much I am relying on you? You are a fine rider, you must keep Stella exercised and fed and prepare her for the day when the war is over and then I will come back and race in the Palio once more."

I sniffled a little. "I don't want you to go."

"Hey, hey now, what's this nonsense? No crying!" Carlo brushed away the tears on my cheek.

"Loretta," he said. "I have not told you the most important part yet. It is not just the horses who are relying on you. There is a very important task that I must ask you to do for me. While we are hiding in the forest you will be our courier. It is a very dangerous and serious job, for unless you bring us food we will starve out there. The Nazis won't suspect a young girl of being an agent for the freedom fighters. You can carry supplies and messages in and out of our camp without getting caught."

I felt my spirits leap at this. I would still be able to see my brother! Also, Carlo was entrusting me with the most important mission. I was to be the go-between, the vital link between the freedom fighters and the outside world.

I fought back my tears. I was working for the freedom fighters now and blubbing was not appropriate. "I will be a trustworthy courier," I told him, bravely jutting out my jaw, feeling the weight of the role he had assigned me resting heavy on my young shoulders.

"Good girl!" Carlo smiled.

The tap-tap of pebbles being flicked onto Carlo's bedroom window startled both of us at that moment. I peered down warily at three dark shapes in the garden below. It was Arturo, Gino and Vincenzo.

"They are here for me," Carlo stood up from the bed and threw his duffel bag over his shoulder. "I have to go now, Loretta. Don't worry, I will see you soon!"

As he got up to go, Ludo leapt up with him.

"No, Ludo," Carlo said. "You must stay with Loretta."

"You aren't taking him with you?"

"Ludo cannot come." Carlo was firm. "I can't feed him and care for him out there. It is better for him to remain here."

Ludo cocked his head to one side and gave a whimper, as if he knew at that moment that Carlo was leaving him, and I felt the tears prick my eyes once more, not for myself this time but for poor Ludo.

Some dogs belong to the whole family and will take a pat or a bone from whoever wants to give it. But Ludo was not like that. The dog had just one master, my brother. He was the most devoted of companions, always accompanying Carlo out hunting or riding. If he ever got left behind, Ludo would wander disconsolately from room to room, looking out of the windows and waiting for Carlo to come back again, then greeting him joyously, leaping up and licking him.

Poor Ludo. I think he howled louder than me that night. He paced back and forth until he had almost worn a groove in the floorboards of my bedroom. Finally, he fell asleep on the hard floor, but even in his dreams I could hear his whimpers of distress.

"Don't cry, Ludo." I stroked his shaggy coat. "We will both see him again soon, I promise."

Carlo had entrusted me to be the courier. It was a top-secret mission.

"So secret that you cannot tell anyone," I said to Marco.

I had to tell Marco of course, I told Marco everything.

I wanted so badly to tell Mama the truth about my friendship with Marco, but her hatred of the Istrice was so heartfelt, I feared what she would do if I confessed to it.

In public, Marco and I continued to ignore each other, but in private we were closer than ever. Our abandoned villa had become a retreat, from the awfulness of the war. We would meet there as often as we could. Both of us would smuggle morsels of food and we had a deck of cards and would spend hours together, playing, laughing and talking, happy in each other's company.

"I can help the freedom fighters too," Marco offered. "I'll come with you tonight."

"No," I told him. "Too many of us wandering about the woods and the Nazis might get suspicious. I must do this alone."

The truth was, I didn't want to share the job of courier. It made me feel important that Carlo had entrusted me with the role and it was mine and mine alone.

All my life I had hunted and played in the woods that surrounded our villa and I knew them like the back of my hand. But Carlo had gone deeper into the woods than we had ever been in our games or hunts. To journey to his camp I would have to chart a course into the darkest and most remote parts of the forest.

I could never have done it on my own, but luckily I had Ludo. The first time I went, I relied on him entirely. Beyond the point where the paths were familiar Ludo picked up Carlo's scent, his tail shot straight up in the air and he was off and running. I had put him on a lead so as not to lose him as he scampered up and down steep banks and gullies tracking the scent this way and that. His urgency to reach Carlo meant that he dragged me until I fell more than once, so I was covered in muck and leaves by the time I reached the camp.

On that first visit I took a backpack laden with cheese,

meats, bread and fruit, which made it even harder to keep my balance sliding and scrambling after Ludo, but it was worth it for I was an instant hero. There were whoops of delight from Carlo and his friends as they fell upon the food, ripping it to bits like ravenous animals.

"Is there more?" Carlo looked hopefully in the bag.

I shook my head. "This was all I could carry," I said. "But I will come back as often as I can and I will bring some wine too next time."

"Wait!" Carlo said as I stood up to go. "I have a note. Will you take it please to the Prior at the Contrada of the Wolf?"

I looked at the note, and saw that it was written in code.

"Do I need to eat it if I am captured by the Nazis?" I asked.

Carlo smiled. "Good thinking, Loretta. That is why I chose you as our courier."

I ran home through the woods that night, my skin vibrating with the excitement of fulfilling my first mission.

When I reached the door of the Contrada of the Wolf with Ludo still at my side, I caught my breath for a moment then banged on the door with my fist. The Prior himself answered. He peered out suspiciously as if he thought someone might have been following me and then dragged me inside.

"Quickly, Loretta, do not dawdle on the street," he hissed. "And perhaps use the rear entrance next time, yes?"

The Prior was not an old man back then, Piccolina. He was only perhaps twenty, very young to be in charge of the Lupa contrada, but then there was a war on so most of the older men had gone to fight. The Prior had flat feet and this defect apparently meant he was not allowed to join the army. He also had the trust of the fascists who thought he was one of them. He had so far managed to evade suspicion, when in fact he was working with the freedom fighters.

I was never aware of the contents of the messages I gave to the Prior. I did not read code and I think Carlo thought it best if I never knew what the notes were about. That way, if I was stopped and questioned by the Blackshirts, I would not know anything, and of course I would have eaten the note. I had practised this at home with a piece of paper, and while I nearly gagged at first,

I did manage to chew and swallow, so I knew if the time came I could do it.

As for the packages that the Prior gave me to ferry to my brother, I did not ask what was inside. There was this one time, though, when the package ripped on a tree branch and I found myself unable to resist the urge and took a peek beneath the brown paper and saw three passports. I took them out to look at them. The pictures in the passports looked like Signora Garo and her children, but their names were different – it said she was Esmeralda Garibaldi!

Of course the passports were fakes and the freedom fighters were smuggling out people who were in trouble with the Blackshirts, helping them to get to the coast.

As summer became winter, I took all the warm blankets and coats that I could manage to round up out into the forest. Carlo and his men's numbers had swelled by now – there were almost a dozen of them. Every few weeks they would move their camp to a new location in the forest. It was a precaution, Carlo said, to make sure that the Blackshirts could not find them. I never had trouble finding their new camp though because Ludo always scented out Carlo and located him for me. He always came with me on my journeys back and forth through the forest, although he howled every time he had to leave Carlo's side and return home with me. At the villa each night Ludo would sleep at the foot of my bed, but he never laid his head on my lap or followed me around the house the way he had done with Carlo. He was still my brother's dog and he made it clear every day in little ways that his loyalty was unswerving. At night, sometimes I would wake up to find him staring out of the window, as if he knew that his master was out there and he longed to be with him.

Stella was a different matter. I had always clicked with the mare right from the start, and she was happy with me on her back as we began to train in earnest. The summer had been and gone and there had been no Palio for the third time in a row, but I was determined that if it was run again next year then Stella would be ready for Carlo to ride when he returned.

With my father and brother both gone, I was left in charge of the training regime. I took it seriously, making a wall chart of the days, noting the progress of each horse and experimenting with various routines. At first, I took a traditional approach, galloping them around and around until they started blowing, with their flanks working like bellows and then taking them home, hosing them off and putting them back in their stalls until the next time.

After a week or two of sticking to the same regime, I found myself bored to tears. Also my muscles were stiff and sore from repeatedly riding the same way. Then a thought struck me. What if the horses felt the same way that I did? What if they were bored with always riding the same routine? And what if their muscles ached too from the stress of galloping day in and day out?

And so I began to devise a training programme of my own. I would gallop on the track one day and then the next we would go out for a long, slow hack, walking up into the hills, letting them stretch their tired muscles and lengthen their necks.

Marco always came with me. I needed him to ride Serafina while I rode Stella. We would ride out for three or four hours some days, chattering away about everything and anything while the horses loped along. As the spring arrived and the trees began to bud green, we would try and see how many different species of trees or flowers we could name. Then, when the summer came and the days grew hot, we would hack out over different paths that led to a natural waterfall and we would ride the horses into the water and swim on their backs, laughing and having splashing fights with each other before sunbathing ourselves dry again and riding home.

Of course I was trying to mix up the training programme – I also had days when I did interval training with Stella, trotting her for five minutes and then cantering for four, then walking for five and so on around the track. My rides with Marco were twice weekly, as my training regime allowed, on a Monday and a Thursday. I didn't really think about it at first, but one Sunday night as I was getting ready for bed I found myself getting quite excited about the fact that tomorrow was a Monday and that meant I would be seeing Marco, and I spent far longer than usual that night at my dressing table in front of the mirror, brushing and brushing my long dark hair until it shone and then plaiting it in braids on either side of my head, and binding them with ribbons.

I'll wear it like this tomorrow, I said to myself. *Marco likes it when I braid my hair...*

And there it was. At that moment I realised with a sudden jolt. How had I not noticed it when it was right in front of my face all along?

I cared what Marco thought. I wanted to look pretty for him.

That dark-eyed, pale-skinned boy with his quiet smile and his quick wit was no longer simply my best friend. I wanted him to be my boyfriend. I had fallen in love.

Terra in the Piazza

Nonna stopped her story abruptly, her cheeks blushing pink like a schoolgirl. "Oh, poor Piccolina! What am I thinking? You do not want to hear such romantic foolishness from your own grandmother!"

"No, Nonna!" I said. "I do want to hear about it. Really, please."

Nonna took my hand, clutching it tight. "I knew Marco and I were star-crossed from the very beginning, but a young heart beats so strong and so certain…"

Then she seemed to change her mind and gave my hand a brisk pat and stood up. "Anyway, no more of such nonsense. I have said enough. I am going to make us some pasta for lunch…"

For the rest of the week whenever I tried to get Nonna to tell me more about Marco she would find an excuse to scuttle out of the room, claiming that she had left the oven on or the tap running. If I had her attention and there was no excuse to get away she would blatantly change the subject. She didn't want to talk about it any more and my dad always said Nonna was harder to move than a half a ton of horse once she made her mind up.

At least she didn't mind that I was spending all my time over at Frannie's. I would walk over to the castle most mornings at around eight and Antonia, Umberto and Leonardo always arrived not long after me, greeting me in the Italian fashion with kisses on both cheeks. "Always the left cheek first!" Antonia taught me.

Before we rode, Violetta would bring breakfast down to the yard and we would all sit together on the hay bales, the warm sweet smell of coffee and rolls mingling with the damp undertones of horse manure and sweat, and I would feel like I was one of the jockeys back home in the bodega.

"All the jockeys in New York ever talk about is how much they weigh and how they got their battle scars," I told the others.

"You want to see my scar?" Antonia said, pulling up her jodhpurs so we could see her ankle. "I had this lovely grey horse. You remember her, Umberto? Trieste, her name was. She was a grand prix showjumper. I was showjumping her at the time when this happened. Halfway through the round a dog runs onto the course and Trieste goes straight up in a rear. When I fell off she panicked and came down on top of me with her front legs and crushed my ankle. I've got plate steel and six screws in there."

"Does it hurt?" I asked.

"It tingles whenever it rains," Antonia shrugged, "but it hardly ever rains in Siena, so no, not much."

"I broke my collarbone." Leonardo pulled down the neck of his shirt so that I could see how it had healed crooked.

Frannie frowned. "I don't remember that."

"It was a car accident," Leonardo told us.

Umberto threw his panino at him. "Doesn't count!" he groaned.

190

"Have you ever broken anything, Lola?" Antonia asked.

Yes, I broke a nose once – only it wasn't mine.

"No," I said, deciding against going into the whole Jake Mayo story, "but my dad has broken loads of stuff." And I told them about the finger he cut off with the axe, which drew the appropriate cries of horror and disbelief.

"No way!" Frannie was laughing.

"It's true!" I insisted. "You can ask my nonna."

I'd always thought that the jockeys at the bodega were trying to out-tough each other with their tales, but as we all sat there eating buttered rolls and charting our injuries, I realised that it was the stories of hot, crazy, difficult horses that were the key to it all. We loved talking about horses in the same way that the kids at school might have talked for hours about skateboarding tricks or what music they were listening to. I would pretend to care about that stuff, but I didn't have anything to say. Here in Italy, though, they spoke the same language as me – they talked horse.

Of the four of them, Antonia was the best all-round horseman. She was the one who would poultice a hoof if there was a stone bruise, or talk to Signor Fratelli about making changes to the training regime if she thought a horse was underperforming in his workouts. She always took the lead and set the pace every time we rode out, which is why it was so surprising when she told me she had no wish to ride the Palio.

"There is no great secret to it," Antonia said when I asked her why she didn't want to race. "I just don't think I'm cut out for it. I like to train the horses, but the idea of being out there with all those other jockeys trying to kill me and my horse, and the pressure and all those people watching us…" She gave a dramatic shiver. "I'm not brave enough. I knew long ago I would not be a fantino. But I love training. One day I would like to have my own stables like Signor Fratelli."

Signor Fratelli reminded me of Nonna the way he ran his stables. He knew every horse intimately. Each morning when they were led into the yard he would examine them, feeling their legs as he chatted away briskly in Italian to the riders, asking how their previous workouts had been, whether the horses felt fresh or tired, discussing feeding and supplements.

He gave very detailed instructions to Frannie, Leonardo, Umberto, and Antonia. I would stand there waiting my turn, but it never came. Signor Fratelli totally blanked me every time. He would walk straight past me and Nico without a single word of encouragement or advice. He would never even look at me and yet there were times when I would be in the yard with Nico and I would get this feeling like the hairs on the back of my neck were standing on end and I would look around and see Signor Fratelli just standing there staring at me. It reminded me of the way the Prior had eyeballed me just before he chased me with his scissors in the Via di Vallerozzi.

"Your granddad doesn't like me," I told Frannie.

"Of course he does!" Frannie said. "His English is poor, that's all. He lets you ride Nico, doesn't he?"

Ever since that first ride when we had overtaken Antonia I had become the only one that Signor Fratelli would allow on Nico's back.

I hoped Signor Fratelli hadn't been watching us too closely on the early workouts. It had taken me time to get used to riding without a saddle. At home we rode in jockey pads, our stirrups raised right up so that we virtually perched above the horse's back. It was so foreign to me to have no saddle at all and I noticed that while the others rode with their legs hanging long, I still rode like an American jockey, my knees tucked up high, my torso tilted forward over Nico's neck. Nico seemed to like this. The way I sat, with my weight above his withers, gave him a chance to let his strides roll and use his back to drive his haunches. The more I rode him, the more I was feeling the raw power of him. It was like he had been holding back that first day, taking it easy on me. Now, with each ride, I could feel him letting go more and more, and I began taking risks, testing the boundaries, pushing him to gallop into the curve of the corner, riding him hard on the straight to see just how much speed he had in him. We were starting to gel, and I knew it was in part because Signor Fratelli had given us the chance to be together exclusively, cementing the bond between us.

All the same, every time I arrived at the stables I would be anxious until I saw my name beside Nico's on the white board, just in case Signor Fratelli had changed his mind and assigned my horse to another rider. The white board was hung on the wall of the stables with details on the workouts we were to ride each day. The riders were listed beside the horse chosen for them and my name would always be written alongside Nico's in green pen. Until we reached August the thirteenth. On this date the green pen was gone and so was my name. Nico was listed without a rider noted beside him and there were words written alongside in the calendar margin. They said: *La Terra in Piazza.*

"It means dirt in the town square," Frannie translated. "It's the day that they truck in the soil and spread it out over the piazza ready for the Palio."

"But I thought the Palio was run on the sixteenth?"

"It is," Umberto said. "But for two days beforehand they will have trials in the square. The fantinos come and ride their best horses in the hope that they will be chosen to race for the contradas."

"So Nico will be ridden in the square by a real fantino?" I felt as if someone had crushed all the air out of me.

"It is no better for me," Umberto sighed. "The best fantinos will step up and get their pick of the horses. Signor Fratelli is the trainer but he is forced to do whatever the Capitano of the contrada demands. They will hand over Dante to another fantino with more experience than me, I am certain. I will get given the second-rate horses to ride – if I get one at all."

"I can't believe you!" It was Leonardo. "Both of you, waiting for the contradas to take your horses from you! Where is your fight?"

Umberto glared at him. "Seriously. What do you expect me to do?"

Leonardo looked uncertain, and now it was Frannie who spoke up.

"We ride the night trial on the fourteenth. All of us. We'll take the horses to the piazza tomorrow night."

"All of us?" Antonia had been ignoring the conversation until this point, but now she had woken up. "I suppose it's not like a real race," she said sounding slightly nervous at the prospect.

"It's a training race," Frannie reassured her.

"Grandfather is planning to enter the horses anyway, why not let us ride them?"

"It makes sense," Leonardo agreed. "Amateurs are allowed in the night trials."

"I'm not an amateur," Umberto said sniffily. "I'm an apprentice."

"After tomorrow night you may not be an apprentice any more," Leonardo said. "If a Capitano chooses you then you might be able to call yourself a fantino at last."

"You aren't hungry, Lola?" Nonna noticed as I picked at my ravioli. "What's the matter?"

On the way home from Frannie's, the grim realisation had set in. Despite all of Leonardo and Frannie's big talk, the truth was I was no fantino – I was a twelve-year-old kid from Ozone Park. Nico was going to be taken away from me and handed over to a proper fantino to ride.

"Nothing."

"Come on, Lola," Nonna said. "Something is wrong, I know it. Talk to me."

I took a deep breath. "Nonna? You remember

how you told me that Stella felt right from the start like she was your horse? Were you ever jealous that someone else was going to ride her?"

Nonna rested her fork on her plate. "Lola, you have grown up with racehorses. You know how the business works. We devote ourselves to them and care for them, but we can never, ever own them and the decisions over their fate are not ours to make."

"I know," I said. "But it's not fair…"

"No," Nonna agreed. "It is even worse because often the owners, they know nothing about horses. They watch a race and they don't understand the tactics or the training or the big picture. If they see their horse lose then they leap to lay blame on the trainer or the jockey and the next thing you know that horse has a new rider and you are on the trash heap. This is the business we are in, Lola. You cannot afford to become attached to a particular horse, only to have it snatched away from you and given to someone else."

"Yes, Nonna," I said. "I know all of that, but –"

"But," my nonna continued, "despite all of this, and against all common sense, sometimes you will find yourself a horse that is special, that holds a place in your heart above all the rest. And when that happens you will know in your bones, that no matter what, you are the only person who should ride her. It is as if you are two parts of a whole and you are destined to be joined together."

I felt a lump in my throat and I gulped it down.

Nonna took my hand. "So, are you going to tell me about this horse who has you all tied up in knots then?"

"It's Nico," I said. "He's a horse at Frannie's stables. The big chestnut I was telling you about."

"I thought you had been given him to train?"

"I have. But the Palio is in two days now and they're going to take him off me and give him to a fantino to ride in the race and…"

Nonna saw the tears welling in my eyes.

"Oh, my Piccolina! And it breaks your heart just to think of someone else riding him instead of you?"

I nodded, gulping down my childish tears.

"Have you ever felt like that, Nonna?"

My nonna went quiet for moment and then she

said. "Once, Piccolina. But that was a very long time ago."

"Was it Stella?"

"It was," Nonna Loretta said. "Carlo had left her in my care, you see, and I had grown to love her so deeply. But it was different with me and Stella. I never expected her to be mine."

"What happened, Nonna?"

I saw the pain in my grandmother's eyes.

"Piccolina," she said. "I have never spoken of this to anyone, not even to your father…"

She clutched at my hand and held it tight. "I told you that I had come home to Italy because it was time at last for forgiveness? But can anyone truly expect to be forgiven for causing the death of someone they love?"

Nonna wiped a tear from her eye. "It was so long ago, but my memory is so clear of the very last time I saw him. It should have been a day of glory. August the sixteenth, 1944, the day of the Palio. Instead, it was to be the day that I lost him for ever…"

Betrayal

I didn't know what to do about Marco. How do you tell a boy that you are suddenly out-of-the-blue in love with him? Ever since we were six years old our friendship had been so natural and easy and now I was like a different person when I was in his company. I found myself giggling and preening around him, acting awkward and strange.

Marco, for his part, was completely oblivious to my feelings. And he didn't seem to appreciate my efforts to turn myself into a beguiling seductress.

"Why is your face so pink? Are you hot?" he asked me.

"You don't like it?"

Marco frowned. "Your lips have gone a funny colour too. Maybe you're getting sick?"

Out of his sight, in the stables, I rubbed my cheeks

furiously with damp fingers to get rid of the rouge and bit at my lips to chew off the crimson stain I had so painstakingly applied that morning.

When I stole some of my mother's expensive perfume Marco complained that there was a "weird smell in the stables" and that perhaps Ludo had brought in a rat and it had died. My efforts to replace my trousers with pretty dresses caused bafflement.

"How can you ride in that?" Marco asked me. "Isn't it uncomfortable?"

At the time when he asked me this question I was struggling to stay on Stella's back as my flouncy floral skirt kept flying up and exposing my knickers. I had tried tucking it in under my thighs, but this was impossible and I couldn't even trot and had to stick to a walk. By the time we got back to the stables after a very unsuccessful training session, Marco was furious with me.

"You slowed us down out there. I don't know what's wrong with you!" he fumed.

"What's wrong with me?" I shot back. "What about you? Telling me I smell like a dead rat and that my lipstick makes me look ill!"

Marco's frown deepened. "That smell was you?"

"It was French perfume!" I snarled.

"Well, why are you wearing perfume to the stables?" Marco snapped back.

"For you!" I shouted.

I had turned bright pink and this time it was not make-up. Marco stared at me, open-mouthed, I could see his brain processing what I had just told him.

"Oh." That was all he said.

My humiliation was complete.

"I need to go," I mumbled and I turned and ran out of the yard.

"Loretta!" I heard him running after me, and the next thing I knew he had grabbed me by the shoulders and was turning me to face him.

"You've been doing this for me?"

"Don't!" I was almost in tears. "Don't make me feel more stupid than I already do! I am so embarrassed! Can we please just forget this ever happened?"

"No," Marco said. "We can't." And his arms closed tight around me and the next moment he was kissing me. It was the best kiss in the world and as he stood back and let me go he said, "I don't think it is you, I really think there might be a dead rat in the stables."

People will tell you that falling in love is the most wonderful feeling in the world. It is not. Falling in love is sickening, like a roller-coaster ride on an empty stomach. But being loved back, that is incredible. It sounds so terrible to say that 1944, the year when all around us lives were being destroyed by war, was a joyful time. But for Marco and me it was truly happy. In a way, I do not know if our love could have existed without the war. Our families had been turned upside down and the chaos made our relationship possible. Who was going to notice a hidden romance between a girl from Lupa and a boy from Istrice when there were Nazi troops marching their way into the countryside and the fascists were hunting down freedom fighters and putting them on trial as criminals?

"All the same," Marco said, "we must be careful. Your family and mine would not approve if they knew."

"They will have to know eventually, won't they?"

We were out riding on Serafina and Stella. It was a gloriously sunny day and I was having trouble holding Stella to a walk, she was keen to gallop and so was I. I kept the reins taut, rather enjoying the way she jogged impatiently, springing along with her head held high.

Marco went silent for a moment and then he said, "If

we tell them we are in love they will never accept that we should be together..."

I was dismayed until he added, "...but if we were married, then surely they'd have no choice."

There were a thousand butterfly wings pounding inside my chest, this overwhelming sense of pure happiness lifting me up, up into the sky.

"You want to get married?"

"That is what I just said, Loretta," Marco said softly. "I want to marry you. Do you want to marry me?"

I thought about this for a moment. This was a real marriage proposal and although I was only fifteen I knew it was serious.

"Would our children be raised as Lupa or as Istrice?"

"They would be raised as our children and we would love them together as a family," Marco said. "To me that would be all that would matter."

"And when would the wedding be?"

"After the war is over. In spring. In the chapel on the outskirts of the city."

"And what sort of flowers would I carry?"

"Loretta!" Marco laughed. "You are being difficult now and you have still not given me your answer. Are you going to marry me or not?"

That night, back at the stables, I spent a long time alone with my horse, brushing her and putting a braid in her mane. "This is how you will wear it for my wedding day," I whispered to her. "I am getting married, Stella. What do you think of that?"

By 1944 the piazza, where we had once thrilled to the sound of racing hooves, had become a haunted place. The fascists had set up their headquarters in the mayor's chambers and no one wanted to go anywhere near, for even looking at a Blackshirt the wrong way, or whispering to a friend in the street might be enough to see you dragged into their rooms and "questioned" for hours. Some men who were taken away for interrogation were never seen again.

The horror stories that Marco had once told me when we were young children about castor oil and beatings were true, and they were nothing compared to the cruelties that the fascists dished out now that their power base was crumbling. As more and more young Italians chose to join the freedom fighters, and the Nazis rode into town on tanks, the fascists were beset from both sides, trying to crush the rebellion and to keep control from the Germans.

One day I came home from the market and told Mama about a poster on the wall of the town hall.

"The Blackshirts have put it there, and it lists crimes and punishments," I said.

"What crimes?" Mama asked nervously.

"Stealing food, disobeying curfew and failing to salute the Nazi troops," I told her.

Mama said nothing. She knew we were guilty of all of these crimes. Everyone stole food now – how else could we possibly survive? We were starving and the Nazis would come and grab from us what little supplies we had. Our cow had been taken from us long ago and then last week the Germans took Gertie, our milking goat, too. We had no vegetables in the garden and no grain to make bread. Without Carlo to hunt for us there was no meat to put on the table. Theft was all we had left. As for saluting the Nazis – we saluted their faces, but as soon as their backs were turned we would spit in the streets after them.

The last crime on the list was separate from the rest and printed in bold, black type:

Anyone who assists or hides the "freedom fighters" will be punished by death without trial.

"Loretta. I cannot let you do this."

Marco blocked the doorway of the stables. "The Nazis are everywhere and the Blackshirts too. It is too dangerous to go into the woods. Show me the path, give me directions and I will go instead."

"No!" I was horrified. "I can't let you take the risk. He is my brother."

"Then at least let me come with you?"

I shook my head. "It is safer if I go alone. If there are two of us there is more chance of attracting the attention of the Nazi soldiers."

"I am begging you, Loretta, please don't go."

I threw the backpack over my shoulder and gave Marco a kiss. "I must. I will be back before dawn, I promise."

As I walked along the Via di Vallerozzi that evening, I heard the bells in the tower chime and I knew it was almost nine. In one hour's time it would be curfew and if the Blackshirts caught me out on the streets I would be taken away. I had to hurry.

Outside the Contrada of the Lupa I looked left and right

to check that there was no one watching me before I gave the secret code – four knocks on the door followed by four more. There were footsteps inside and then a moment later the door swung open and there was the Prior.

"You are late," he hissed as he handed me the package.

It was wrapped in brown paper. I had no idea what was inside but I knew better than to ask. I shoved it inside my backpack. At my feet, Ludo gave an anxious whine as if to say, "We should get going".

I was about to leave when I noticed the bruises on the Prior's face.

"What happened to you?" I asked.

"Nazi soldiers were here earlier today," the Prior said. "They... asked me a few questions."

He seemed shaken, and I noticed that his hand that held the door was trembling.

"They beat you? What did they want to know?"

The Prior looked past my shoulder and checked anxiously up and down the Via di Vallerozzi.

"You should not dwell here on the doorstep," he said. "It would be bad for us both if the Nazis were to find us like this. Go to your brother, Loretta, no more questions!"

We were clear of the city before the bell tolled for

curfew. That night there was a full moon, which was good because it made it easier for me to see once we had left the lamplights behind. Although by the time Ludo and I were actually inside the forest it was so dark we could barely make out the path. I relied on the dog to lead me as he had done so many times before, his instinct for sniffing out Carlo remained as strong as it had ever been.

We had been walking for about half an hour when I heard voices. Not Carlo and his men, but other voices, coming towards me. With my heart pounding I grabbed Ludo to me and flung myself down into the undergrowth.

"Ludo, please! Shhh."

Ludo was growling. A low, protective growl – the sort of growl that a dog instinctively gives when there is an intruder.

"No!" I hissed at him. "You must be quiet!" I wrapped my hand tight around his jaw and he stopped growling, as if he knew that it was a matter of life and death. Just as he did so I saw the men, a patrol of five Blackshirts. They were walking along, their guns hanging at their waists, cigarettes in their hands. They were talking about their girlfriends. One of them was complaining that she didn't cook spaghetti as well as his mother and then another Blackshirt said that although his girlfriend was an excellent cook, she nagged him terribly and which was worse? All this time I was lying on my belly on the cold, damp, rotten leaves with my arms wrapped tight around Ludo. I was so certain that at any moment they were going to hear me because in my ears my breathing was as loud as a jet plane and my heart was beating so hard it was like a kettle drum. The men had stopped! They were standing right there next to us. I felt a growl rising in Ludo's chest and I held my breath. *Please no, Ludo, please.*

And then... nothing. The men began to walk again. I heard their voices receding, moving away from me down the path towards the city and then the air was silent and empty once more. I stayed lying there, face down, for what seemed like an eternity until I was certain that they had gone. Then I got to my feet and I ran.

I ran in the dark, Ludo leading me, tumbling down banks and pushing my way through the undergrowth. By the time I reached Carlo's camp, almost an hour later, I was sobbing and shaking like a leaf.

"Hey, hey." Carlo hugged me tight. "You are OK now,

Loretta. Everything is OK."

I couldn't speak. My words kept getting stuck in my throat, and it was taking all my effort just to gulp down air, hyperventilating and gasping for breath.

"You are certain that they went the other way?" one of the freedom fighters asked me. "The Blackshirts? They went back towards town?"

"Yes," I said. Although even as I said this I realised I was not completely certain. I hadn't dared to move when I was lying there on the ground with Ludo. I had heard the voices fading but I wasn't sure what direction the men had taken exactly.

"I have something for you," I told Carlo. "From the Prior."

I handed him the package from my backpack and also a block of cheese and a loaf of bread, which, considering how hungry I was, felt like handing over gold bullion, but I knew that Carlo and his men were starving.

"Do you want coffee?" Carlo asked me. "It will warm you up. Here, sit down!"

I sat down on a fallen log beside the open fire and warmed myself while Carlo poured me a drink.

"You are very brave, Loretta," my brother said. "I know

it is more dangerous than before to come here." He ruffled my hair and then he said, "Loretta my little *Scavezzecolla*. How are the horses? How is Stella?"

"She is fit," I said, "and sound. Ready to run the Palio."

"Good, good!" Carlo said. "I knew I could count on you, Loretta. She is a great horse. You must keep her safe for me until I come home, yes? Until I return no one else can ride her, Loretta, only you. You understand?"

I nodded and took a sip of coffee. The warmth of it in my stomach made me bold.

"I have news to tell you," I said.

"What is it?"

Another sip and then I spoke. "Marco has asked me to marry him. We are engaged."

For two weeks now, ever since Marco had asked me to be his bride, I had been dying to tell Carlo. I had thought about this moment, fondly imagining his reaction. What I did not anticipate was the utter fury that confronted me as his face darkened and he began to rage.

"No!" he shouted, raising his voice so that the other men in the camp came rushing to see what was wrong. "Out of the question, Loretta! Forget about it! It will never happen!"

"But..." I stammered. "I thought you would be happy for me!"

"Happy for you to destroy our family by marrying some filthy Porcupine!"

"You told me that you didn't care about contradas – that they don't matter!" I cried.

"You can be friends with him – sure!" Carlo shouted. "But marrying him is another matter! You will break Mama's heart! Do you know what you are doing? If you marry a Porcupine then you will be disowned by the Lupa contrada. You will be an outcast! Did you ever think about that?"

"You, of all people, Carlo!" I shouted at him. "I thought you would understand. You should be happy for me."

Carlo shook his head. "I cannot be happy for you, Loretta, when you are making the wrong decision. A marriage between a Wolf and a Porcupine will end in disaster. It cannot happen."

"Well, it is going to happen," I told him as I flung my backpack over my shoulders. "And when I walk up the aisle I will do it alone, without you to hold my hand because you are no longer my brother!"

"Loretta!" Carlo shouted after me, but I turned my back

on him and left the campsite in floods of tears, running alone through the woods. Ludo, who had been whimpering while we fought, remained loyal to my brother as always, abandoning me to stay behind at his master's feet.

No longer my brother. I have regretted my bitter, cruel words now for seventy years, for they were the last I ever spoke to Carlo.

The troop of Blackshirts that I thought I had so cleverly avoided in the forest that night had not gone back to town. They had followed me, silently, patiently stalking my every step, until I led them right to where they wanted to go.

When they stormed the camp it was bedlam. Two of the freedom fighters were killed that night. The rest were captured by the Blackshirts and forced at gunpoint back into Siena. In the mayor's chamber they interrogated them. My brother was beaten until he was unconscious. They cut him and electrocuted him and spat on him and abused him and tried to make him talk and then, when he refused to tell them what he knew, they dragged him to the piazza where they had erected the gallows for all to see.

I didn't go to watch the public hanging. I did not want

the memory of my brother to be stained by those final, brutal moments as the rope caught his weight and his neck snapped.

That is how my brother's life came to an end. Hanged as a traitor. And I, the girl who led the Blackshirts straight to him, have lived with the guilt and horror of the ultimate betrayal all my wretched life.

Night Trials

It's not your fault. I told Nonna that. I said she couldn't have possibly known the Blackshirts were following her, that it was an accident. But I knew how hollow my words were to her. If it had been Johnny or Vincent who'd got killed because of something I had done, no matter what anyone said, I would have felt the same way.

When Nonna had spoken about forgiveness, I thought she had been angry at the Prior. It never occurred to me that it was her. That she was the one who needed to be forgiven.

"The Prior knew about what happened that night?" I asked.

Nonna nodded. "He told me to be quiet about

it. He said that if the people knew I had been the one to lead the Blackshirts to Carlo and the others then they would turn the blame against me. He convinced me it wasn't going to do any good, so I didn't tell, not even Mama. I pushed it down inside me and I never spoke of it. Only Marco knew my secret and he swore he would tell no one. When my father came home Mama told him that Carlo had been tortured and killed by the Blackshirts and I said nothing…"

"Your father came home?" I was surprised.

"Yes, Piccolina," Nonna said. "When the war ended he was released from duty. He made his way home to us, although he nearly died twice on the way back to Italy. Once when his boat was sunk and another time when the Nazi troops boarded his train. He was a changed man when he got home. He had seen so much death on the battlefields and he had long ago lost faith in *Il Duce* and what he had been fighting for. He was proud to hear that Carlo had been a freedom fighter before his death. If only my brother had known this because he believed himself to be on the opposite side of the war to his own father. Italy was so divided then – in our own town neighbours turned against one another as the civil war took its grip. And then in September of 1945 when the announcement came that the war had ended, with it came the news that the Palio would be held once more, and there would be a special Palio to celebrate. They called it the Palio of Peace."

Her eyes welled with tears once more. "I had prepared Stella all this time to be ready to race. If Carlo had still been alive he would have ridden for our contrada. To see the *terra* in the piazza for the first time in five years and for Carlo not to be here…"

The *terra* in the piazza! I had forgotten all about it.

"Nonna," I said. "Right now there is dirt again in the square. Tomorrow they are holding races and Frannie has asked me if I want to ride Nico.

"They are holding the night trials?"

"Yes."

Nonna shook her head, "No, Piccolina. It's too dangerous."

"Frannie says it's not rough, not like the real race."

Nonna looked serious. "And this Frannie, he has seen it all before, has he? He has felt the slam of his bones against the bricks of the buildings when a horse fails to make the turn or the weight of a horse coming down hard on top of his body when it trips and falls? He is an expert on such things, this boy you have only just met? I have ridden the Palio, Lola, it is the most dangerous horse race in the world. The night trials are run on the same track, I cannot let you –"

"Nonna!" I said. "If you don't let me ride Nico then I'm going to lose him. They will give the ride to another fantino if I don't say yes."

I felt my eyes blur with tears. "He's *my* horse, Nonna. It should be me on his back. You told me that you felt the same way once. So you know how I feel and you know you have to let me ride."

Nonna took my hand. "Oh, Piccolina," she sighed. "The trouble is, you have too much of my blood in you. Very well, ride the night trials. But I will come to watch, yes? I want to see this Nico for myself."

*

A jockey spends half their life in the dark. Back home I would watch Johnny and Vincent ride morning workouts at Aqueduct with no lights and nothing but a white rail to their left hand side to use as a guide to stop them from crashing off the track.

Except a white rail is a different story from a wall of solid stone. Also, I wasn't riding a workout in the piazza – this was a race. If I was to win it, I would need to fight all the way to the finish.

"Just try to stay on the inside track and don't let the other fantinos push you around," Leonardo said. He vaulted up onto on his grey gelding, Nuvola, who was fretting and side-stepping anxiously in anticipation. "It is better at night," he added. "At least in the dark you do not see the wall before it strikes you in the face."

"Don't listen to him," Antonia glared at Leonardo. "He's been trying to scare me ever since we got here and now he's trying to mess with you too! The horses can see well enough in the dark. Besides, the walls are not that solid. They pad them you know, with feather mattresses."

I looked around anxiously at the padded walls. Was a feather mattress enough to protect a horse if it crashed at full gallop?

Perhaps it wouldn't be a problem. Frannie hadn't turned up yet with Nico. I didn't even have a horse. I was standing on the track with Leonardo, Umberto and Antonia waiting for him to arrive with just minutes left before the horses were due to run.

It had taken me and Nonna for ever to walk into town. She took such small steps that a walk with her was half-speed and it was a long way. At one point when we sat down on a stone wall so she could take a breather I worried that she wouldn't be able to stand up again.

"I am slowing you down, Piccolina," she said, patting my hand. "You go on ahead without me. I will catch you up."

"Nonna!" I said. "Don't be silly, we have loads of time."

We had made it to the square with only minutes to spare. I'd helped Nonna climb up the stairs to the seating, which had been erected on the top step of the town hall, and then raced into the darkness to find Frannie.

As I ran, I felt the soil, so strange underfoot where the bricks used to be just a day before. It felt just like the Aqueduct racetrack. All around me horses were snorting and stamping anxiously, and there was the smell of sweat and turf in the air. My senses were overwhelmed by the conviction that I was home. I half-expected Johnny and Vincent to emerge from the shadowy ranks of the riders in front of me, messing with each other and cracking jokes like they always did before they rode track.

"Lola? There you are!" Frannie came forward from the darkness. He was mounted up on his horse and leading Nico.

"Better get onboard," he said, passing me Nico's reins. "They're about to get underway."

"Is Signor Fratelli here with you?" Umberto asked him.

"He's here somewhere," Frannie said. "I saw him talking with the Capitano of the Lupa contrada."

"The Lupa contrada are here?"

"All the contradas are here," Frannie replied.

"They all want to see which horses are the fastest."

"How will they see if we're racing in pitch-black darkness?" I asked.

"Ah," Umberto said, finding us along with Leonardo and Antonia. "That is the challenge. We race at night so that secrets can be kept."

"Quickly, Lola!" Frannie said as he held Nico steady while I mounted. "We need to get down there!"

Nico was tense when I got on his back. I could feel his muscles taut and twitching, and he held his head up higher than usual, giving little snorts with each jerky step he took. I stroked his neck as we walked, trying to settle his nerves even though I felt sick with anticipation myself.

Two lamps on either side of the town hall illuminated the start line so that you could make out the silhouettes of the horses and riders as they lined up behind the rope. The rest of the square was in complete darkness. All I could see was the inky outline of the buildings, their solid blackness contrasting against the fuzzy gloom of the night sky above. But at speed on a racetrack?

I would never see them in time. I would have to rely on Nico to be my eyes. I hoped Antonia was right about horses being able to see in the dark.

I looked up at the town hall. I could just make out Nonna tucked away in the back row of the seating where the spectators were gathered. Frannie's grandfather was right upfront in the first row and beside him a man whose jet-black hair, sculpted sideburns and beard gave him the rather disturbingly devilish appearance in the golden lamplight.

"Who's that?" I asked Frannie.

"The Capitano of the Lupa," he replied.

The Capitano was younger than I expected. I had thought he would be an old man, like the Prior. He seemed very intent on looking at all the horses and riders and making notes in a little diary. He cast a long gaze over Nico and for a brief moment I caught his eye. He did not acknowledge me.

"So the Capitano chooses the horse and fantino who will race for Lupa?"

Frannie nodded. "For the Lupa, all decisions are his alone."

"What about the Prior?"

"The Prior is the head of the contrada, but the Capitano is the horseman, in charge of strategy and decisions."

The Capitano had turned to Signor Fratelli. He was pointing out Nico and saying something and now both men had their eyes trained on us.

"They are watching you," Antonia whispered to me.

"They are watching Nico," I corrected her.

A trumpet sounded to signal that it was time to line up. In front of the town hall the two men holding the thick rope that was used to start the race pulled it to bring it taut at waist height.

Nico snorted, nostrils widening at the sight of the rope raising up. He began to step backwards.

"Nico! Don't be silly, it's only a rope," I said. "Stand up!"

Nico began to spin around, turning his rump to the rope and I was suddenly aware of just how powerful he was and how small I was on his back compared to the other fantinos. Did I have the strength to handle him in a race situation now that his blood was up?

"Are you OK?" It was Leonardo, right beside me.

I still had Nico turned in the opposite direction, trying to regain control of him. "They won't start the race until we're all lined up, will they?" I asked.

"Do not count on it!" Leonardo shouted back at me. "Turn him forward! Now!"

As he said this I heard a cry go up and suddenly the rope dropped to the ground.

We were racing. Except I was facing in the wrong direction!

Suddenly aware that he'd been left behind, Nico spun around and launched himself after the others. His hindquarters worked like rocket thrusters, and we were in a gallop straight away from a standstill and closing in on the pack ahead.

In just a few strides we reached the back of the field, but there was no way to move any further. We were jammed there, Nico's nose up against the rump of the horse in front. I could see the rider in front of me rising and falling with his horse's strides, his silhouette in the darkness trailblazing my path. It felt safe to be tucked in behind him;

at least I wouldn't be crashing into buildings. But Nico hated it. He loathed being stuck behind the others, the way it made him cramp up his strides. He had his ears pinned flat back, giving little snorts of indignation. To stay here like this was breaking his spirit and I knew I had to make a move now or my horse would sour on me.

"C'mon, Nico," I said, and I wrapped my legs tight around him. The track was blocked in all directions, so I rode for the inside rail, the shortest route, and created a space for myself by barging the haunches of the horse in front. The rider of the horse, a heavyset man with arms like Christmas hams, looked surprised to find me creeping up alongside him. As we approached the dangerous hairpin turn he raised his whip and I realised he was planning to bring it down on me. I braced myself for the blow, but it never came because the next thing I knew he wasn't there any more!

The horse and the rider both plunged away from me. I figured the horse had tripped, but I couldn't be sure in the dark and I didn't risk looking back.

The way they had disappeared it was as if the night had swallowed them whole.

I could hear the shouts and cries of people running out onto the track and I figured people were rushing out to help him. I thought about stopping myself, but there was nothing I could do for them. *Keep going,* a voice in my head said. Nico didn't seem fazed, he was still galloping strongly. Beneath me, his hooves pounded like drumbeats as he settled into his stride and swept across the ground. We were crushing the distance between us and more of the pack ahead.

At the next corner, we'd got so close to the laggers at the rear that the dirt was being kicked up into our faces from their heels. I knew Nico'd be hating being stuck behind them again and this was the time to make our move.

"Open up, boy," I urged him as we came out of the bend. "You can do it!"

I felt Nico power forward with his hindquarters so that his shoulders stayed straight and he accelerated and flattened out and we pressed down on them, his strides chewing up the space, picking off the pack one by one, working my way to the front.

Nico was galloping hard, but he had even more speed in him than he was showing now and I was waiting, biding my time for the moment when I would ask him to shift up a gear.

We had almost reached the town hall again and I knew the time had come. All I needed to do was give a squeeze and a cluck of my tongue.

"Are you ready, Nico?"

He never got the chance to answer me because at that moment there were men running out into the middle of the track in front of us with flags waving over their heads.

I thought it was some sort of contrada celebration at first until I saw them cross the flags to signal us.

"Stop! Stop!"

They were stopping the race! But why? There were still another two laps to go!

There was shouting and people running all over the track and I realised that this had been going on since that fall in the first lap. It hadn't just been the rider alongside me who had gone down. He'd caused a pile-up and taken four other riders down with him!

Now the fantinos were up on their feet and fighting over who had caused the crash. I saw one jockey swing a punch at another rider and instead of holding him back I saw spectators leaping into the fray to help him fight!

"Cheating Panther! Your horse got in the way on purpose!"

"You're the cheats! People of the Unicorn!"

Whistles were being blown and all around me the riders who had been pulled up because of the chaos on the track were abandoning their horses and running to join in! The crowd kept swelling with more and more people until it was no longer a fight – it was a full-blown riot!

I was so busy watching the fighting, I didn't notice that a man had left the crowds and come to stand beside me. Before I could stop him he had his hands on Nico.

"What are you doing?"

The man stared hard at me. "You ride very

bravely for a girl. Taking on men twice your size on a horse like this, it takes great courage. The way you rode for that last corner, it was as if you had been a fantino for many years, and how old are you?"

"Twelve," I said. I was shaking. He had both hands on Nico's bridle. I couldn't pull away. "Could you please let my horse go. Now."

The man smiled. "Lola…You and I, we need to talk."

He knew my name.

"You are afraid of me?" the man asked.

"I'm not," I shot back, my heart hammering.

"Come, then. We have much to discuss."

And with that, the Capitano of the Lupa took the reins and led us both away into the darkness.

By the time I arrived home at the villa it was three in the morning. I looked for the iron key under the flowerpot and couldn't find it, but then when I tried the front door it was open. I walked inside, tiptoeing past Donatello. I noticed that Nonna had raised his visor. I grasped the metal in my hands and pushed it down again.

"Don't close it."

Nonna was standing on the landing, at the top of the stairs.

"Sorry?"

"The visor. Leave it open. He tells me that he wants to see what is going to happen. These are interesting times for a suit of armour and he doesn't want to miss out on anything."

I pushed the visor back up again and continued up the stairs to her.

"I'm sorry I'm so late, Nonna, I got held up…"

"By the Capitano," Nonna said. "Yes, I saw him talking to you."

"How did you know who he was?"

Nonna laughed as if this was a silly question. "So what did he think of Nico, then? Let me guess. He wants him to race for the Lupa, yes?"

"He does," I confirmed. "We went back to the stables together and he asked Signor Fratelli all about Nico's training regime. Like, everything. He wanted to know about his workouts and feeding, the training schedule…"

"Of course he did," Nonna said. "The Capitano is in charge now. He will make judgement on every detail. It is his job to ensure Nico will win the race and bring glory to the Contrada of the Wolf."

"Do you think he can do it?"

As I asked the question, I felt my stomach clench with anticipation. I knew already that the Capitano believed Nico could win. But I didn't care about his opinion. It was my nonna who mattered. In eighty-five years I don't think she had ever been wrong about a horse.

Nonna was silent for a moment, thoughtful. And then she said, "This Nico of yours. I got a good look at him tonight. He is big and burly. The Palio demands lightness and agility."

I felt utterly crushed. All this time I had been convinced Nico was a champion, had I been kidding myself?

"Then I saw the way he ran down that last stretch, the way he opened up when you asked him to make a move. He had such power in his strides, and such a big heart too. It is the heart that will take him the distance. That is what you look for in a horse, Piccolina. Your Nico, he is very special indeed."

"So you think he can win?" I couldn't believe I was hearing this. "Really? You mean it?"

"He will do it," she grunted. The way she said it, her words so intentionally careless, I knew at that moment that she loved him too.

We went to bed after that. Nonna said I looked tired and we would talk more in the morning. It was true, I was exhausted, but I couldn't sleep.

It bothered me that I had only told my Nonna part of the story. I said that the Capitano wanted Nico to run. I hadn't told her the rest of what happened that night.

I must have dozed off for a couple of hours I guess because when I woke up it was still dark outside. I got dressed, feeling a little vacant and light-headed. Nonna was still asleep when I left the villa. I left her a note on the dining table that said "Gone to buy bread, home soon".

I entered the town through the Porta Ovile and negotiated the maze of streets until I found my way to the piazza. I had expected the stall holders to be there, but the square was empty. I hadn't thought about it, but I guess there was no market today as they were preparing for the Palio.

I walked across the square, staring down at the sand where the hooves of the horses had left their mark the night before. I climbed the stairs of the town hall and then sat on the top step and stared out across the piazza, at the newly erected grandstands and the mattresses strapped to the walls. Everything was ready. Tomorrow night the real race would be run here. I had a choice to make and my time was running out.

When I knocked on the door of the Contrada of the Wolf that morning, I had a taste in my mouth like metal and my palms were damp with sweat. I felt like I was going to be sick. I couldn't believe I was really going to do this.

The door swung open and the Capitano was standing there. "Lola," he said softly. "I knew it would be you. You have come to a decision?"

"Yes," I said. "I have."

I had left home early that morning, but by the time I returned to the villa it was late afternoon. Nonna came to open the door when she heard my footsteps on the gravel.

"Where is the bread then?" she asked.

"What?"

"You left this house to get bread for breakfast and now you are home and it is almost dinner time and you have empty hands," she said.

"Oh," I said. "I'm sorry. The stalls were closed."

"And where have you been all this time?" Nonna asked.

I hesitated. "I spent the day with the Capitano in the piazza. He was teaching me about the Palio, the rules and rituals on the day of the race."

I saw the look on Nonna's face.

"You told me the Capitano chose Nico," she said, "but it is not just the horse, is it Lola?"

"No," I admitted. "He wants me. He has asked me to ride for the Wolf, to be Nico's fantino." My nonna's expression became grave. "And what did you say?"

"I told him yes. But I said I have to check with you. I won't do it if you don't want me to."

"But *you* want this, Piccolina? You want to ride your Nico in the Palio?"

"Of course I do!"

Nonna shook her head. "I am not certain that you understand the seriousness of this. It is one thing to get around the piazza in a practice run, but the real thing is so much more dangerous. It is no ordinary horse race. The risks are so great…"

"But you rode in it, Nonna! I thought you would be proud of me being chosen!"

"Piccolina," Nonna said, "there is so much you do not know about what lies beneath this race. The true brutality of the contradas who will stop at nothing to win it."

She took my hand in hers. "It is late I know, but we need to talk about this. I told you about what happened to my brother. But there is more you should know, about me and Marco and what happened after Carlo's murder. Now,

I think at last the time has come for you to hear the end of my story…"

Love and War

I slept in Stella's stall after Carlo died. I could not bear to be in the house without him. Mama cried all the time, and her tears made me feel even worse. If she had known the truth, that Carlo's death had been my fault, it would have truly broken her heart.

Marco tried to convince me that I was wrong. He said that I did not know for sure that the Blackshirts had followed me that night. But how else would they have found their way to the camp?

"Even if it is true," Marco told me, "this is war, and Carlo knew the risks. You are lucky that they did not kill you too, Loretta. You must stop blaming yourself. Carlo would have wanted you to be happy."

"But that's just the thing!" I cried. "He didn't want me

to be happy! He said I shouldn't marry you! That was what we fought about that night, and now he is gone and I will never have the chance to say I am sorry!"

Marco seized upon my words. "Why would you be sorry? Are you saying that you no longer want to marry me?"

I could not meet his eyes. "Carlo said it would never work for a Wolf to marry a Porcupine."'

"But we are not wolves and porcupines!" Marco shook his head in exasperation. "We are people, Loretta. You love me, don't you?"

"I do," I said.

"Then nothing else should matter," Marco said.

I thought about this. "I cannot tell Mama and Papa, not yet," I said. "They are still grieving over Carlo. I must give them time. Please, Marco?"

Marco sighed. "All right. We will wait."

In truth it was not fear of my parents' disapproval or the contrada that held me back from marrying Marco. It was the belief that I held deep inside myself that Carlo's death had been my fault and I did not deserve to be happy.

When the war ended a few months later there were huge celebrations in the piazza, but I could not join in. I was glad that Hitler and the Nazis had been defeated, but none of it would bring my brother back.

The news of the Palio of Peace caused much excitement after five years with no terra in the piazza. The whole city was wild with excitement and everywhere you looked there were banners flying and people chanting and marching as the preparations for the race got underway.

When the night trials were held, Marco, who had always been the best rider in his contrada, won with ease on Clara.

The other contradas had all appointed their fantinos too – all except for the Lupa.

I had not spoken to the Prior since the day that Carlo had died. He thought it best if we were not seen together, it was too dangerous for both of us if the Blackshirts had realised we were connected. We would catch each other's eye sometimes in church, but nothing more.

It was the eve of the Palio of Peace and the Lupa still did not have a horse or a rider to compete. I had decided that I didn't want to know who they would choose, and so I stayed well clear of the night trials, remaining at home with Stella, grooming her and spending my days and nights in her stall. That was where I was when Mama came to find me.

"The Prior and the Capitano are here," she said. "They are in the house waiting to speak with you."

I followed Mama inside and found both men waiting for me.

"Loretta," the Prior said, "there has been a meeting of the council of the contrada to discuss the Palio."

I was prepared for this. I knew they would come and say that they wanted Stella to run. After all, there was no other horse in the contrada who was faster than her.

"I am sorry," I said. "I am loyal to my contrada but Stella is my brother's horse and this was to be his race. I could not bear to watch anyone else ride her in the piazza."

I could feel my heart pounding. To speak out like this and refuse to give them my horse was such defiance, but I did not care. I knew that Carlo had not wanted a stranger to ride Stella in his place.

"Loretta," the Prior said. "You misunderstand the purpose of our visit. We are not here to ask you to give us the mare. We are here to ask if you will ride."

That night I went into Carlo's bedroom. It hadn't been touched since he died, and I felt like I was intruding to be there without him. I got a chair and climbed up to the top shelf of his wardrobe and took down the box that contained his racing silks. I laid them out on the bed and then, with the reverence of a priest donning his robes, I dressed myself and looked in the mirror. I had hoped to look the part, but instead I looked ridiculous. The silk pyjamas of the fantino were meant to be worn loose, but on my slender frame they sagged and bagged as if I were a child playing dressing-up. I could not do this!

"They are a little big on you."

It was Mama. She was standing in the doorway.

"No matter," she said briskly, stepping over to grab at the sleeve, holding it tight and analysing the situation. "I can alter them. Let me get my pins and I will make a few adjustments. It won't take me long..."

"Mama, no..." I tried to object but she silenced me.

"Loretta, it is a good thing that you do this, I feel it in my heart. Your brother loved you more than anyone in the world. You are the only one he would ever have wanted to ride his horse, and if he were here right now he would say to do this for him, for his memory."

"But you don't realise what happened in the woods that night..." I began.

Mama enveloped me in her arms and hugged me tight.

"Loretta. We cannot change what happened that night. But you can still do justice to the memory of your brother. Ride Stella in the Palio. Bring home victory for your contrada and make Carlo proud."

I had agreed to race, but it was too late for me to ride the night trials. The race itself would be the very first time that Stella entered the piazza.

I would have liked to have prepared her better, but how do you prepare any horse for the spectacle that is the Palio?

On the morning of the race, thousands upon thousands of people were crushed together behind the barriers in the centre of the piazza. In the grandstands people were pressed into every nook and cranny. They hung off the balconies and clambered up awnings. Their cries of jubilation often turned into shouts of anger and fights kept breaking out as the contradas shoved up against one another, jostling for position around the square.

I gripped Stella's reins, using all my strength to hold her as she fretted and stamped at the sight of it all. I wouldn't have blamed her if she had reared or refused to move when confronted with such a sight, but it was a mark of the mare's trust in me that she trembled a little as I asked her to walk into the piazza, but did not shy away.

"It's going to be OK," I told her. "I will be with you all the way."

As we walked out onto the track, the other fantinos did not meet my eye. The Palio, as you know Piccolina, is not a typical horse race. It is important to try and have allies, because you will undoubtedly have enemies who will gang up against you and block you or barge you off-course. Unfortunately for me, I was riding for the Lupa, and our contrada did not make friends easily. All the same, I knew that I had one other fantino that I could count on – and that was Marco.

"When we are on the racetrack I will be riding to win for the Istrice. It is my noble duty to do my best. But if a chance comes to protect you from harm, or to help you, I will take it."

These were Marco's words to me and my pact to him had been the same. Other fantinos might be willing to sacrifice the race if it meant stopping their enemy from winning, but for me and Marco, there was no honour in this. He would be trying to win, just like me, and I expected nothing less.

The noise of the crowd was deafening. I could hear the battle cries of the contradas, chanting for their riders.

I... I... I... ISTRICE!

Lu... Lu... Lu... LUPA!

I looked out at the sea of people and saw the colours of the Contrada of the Wolf, flying on banners around the square. My brother had been here before me, in a moment just like this. He had sat astride Serafina and looked up at the crowds and known that the weight of the whole contrada lay on his young shoulders. Now, it was my turn. Could I be as good as Carlo and prove myself worthy?

At the start rope, Marco and I were forced to split up. He had drawn a position in the middle of the field and already I could see the other fantinos forcing him back, kicking and elbowing him off his line. The Lupa had drawn better. I was on the inside of the track and as I lined up at the rope, Stella gave a snort of anticipation. I hadn't been able to ride my mare in the piazza, but I had trained her for this moment for hour upon hour at home, with Marco helping me on the ground holding the rope as we taught Stella to leap forward at the very moment it fell.

"Just like at home," I whispered to Stella. "Ready, wait for it..."

When the rope was suddenly dropped in front of us, Stella leapt like a gazelle. She responded just as I had schooled her to do, moving into a gallop at such speed that within just a few strides she was right at the front, immediately taking the lead.

Marco had started well too, and he was right up at the front of the field. As we came into the first turn I could hear the roar of the crowds all around me, cheering me on. *Scavezzecolla! Scavezzecolla!*

The first corner is the worst on the course, a hairpin bend, and as we took it I felt Stella wobble a little and we brushed against another rider coming through on the outside of me. I was such an innocent that I actually turned around and apologised! Little did I realise that for the next three laps of the track I would be barged and shoved, even whipped and kicked, by the other riders as they forced their way past me and tried to drive me off the track and into the padded walls of the piazza.

By the end of the first lap, I'd been overtaken by four horses and pushed back to mid-field. This was what I wanted as I did not want to hold the lead the whole way. I tucked Stella in behind the horse on the rails in fifth place and I stayed there, letting my mare match the pace, keeping up with the leaders without letting Stella tire herself. The time would come to make my move, but it was not yet. When I held Stella back, almost letting her slip to the rear of the pack for the first two laps of the track, I could hear the cries of dismay from the Lupa fans in the grandstands. They were furious with me and if my strategy did not pay off then I would pay the price for losing.

On the sidelines I knew the Capitano would be cursing my name, but I knew what I was doing. Stella had the power of a sprinter in those final lengths and I was saving her strength. As long as I could get her clear of the pack with our sights on the finish line in the last lap, then she would not fail me.

We were almost seven horses back, bunched in on the inside of the track when we reached the first bend of the last lap. The horses who'd been the early leaders were flagging, and as I rode Stella into the corner I saw a gap near the rail and I went for it.

I used only my voice to urge her on, shouting against the noise and the wind.

"Stella! This is it! Show them what you can do!"

I knew that my mare was fast, but even I did not expect

the acceleration that came when she found her stride that day. We swept through the riders in front of us as if they were standing still, and by the time we reached the next bend only three horses remained out in front, lying between us and victory.

Marco was one of those ahead of us, his horse powering on, in a strong position. I saw him pass another rider to move up to second place. But I was gaining on them, and the Lupa supporters in the stands were going crazy with excitement as they watched us make our move.

Stella's strides swallowed up the ground, edging us closer and closer to the frontrunners until I was neck and neck with Marco. In front of us was the rider in the colours of the Contrada of the Goose. His horse, a bay with four white socks, was running for all he was worth, but Marco and I were both closing the gap. By the final corner, with the finish line so close, it looked like there would be three of us in it all the way to the wire.

As we took the corner, I was so focused on the track ahead I did not see the fist coming, and I was not prepared for the jolt of the punch as it connected with my ribs.

The Goose fantino had struck me! Not by mistake. He had done it intentionally, a gut-punch that was aimed to knock me clear off my horse. I slipped, sliding sickeningly on Stella's back, and at that moment I felt my clever, clever mare swerve in unison to keep her weight underneath me. Somehow I managed to right myself and get back into stride. I was still onboard. To the left of me there was an angry cry from Marco. He'd seen the Goose hit me and he was so furious he barged him! The Goose was catapulted from his mount's back and crashed headlong into the feather mattress of the wall!

"Go, Loretta!" Marco shouted to me. "It's just you and me! There is no one else now!"

We were both riding hard, pumping arms and legs for all we were worth, our horses giving their all as we approached the finish.

As we came to the line, I did not dare to even cast a glance at Marco. The race was too close and even the tilt of my head might have been enough to throw us off and hold us back in the vital rush to the line. All I could do was ride on and exhort Stella to go as fast as she could, and hope that my faith in my horse was proved right.

When we flew across the finish line the cries of the contradas were deafening in my ears, but I still did not know if they were shouts of joy or anguish, until the crowds had raced out onto the track and they were swarming around Stella and hugging her and I had been ripped off her back and I was thrown about like a plaything, over the heads and shoulders of the people as they cried out my name. *Scavezzecolla! Brava, Scavezzecolla!*

I had won.

I know I should have been delighted, but at that moment, swamped in the heaving mass of humanity, my only emotion was raw fear. The crowd fell upon us, threatening to crush us in their frenzy and my poor, brave black mare, exhausted by the race, found herself surrounded by a mob clawing at her and shouting in her face. I could see the terror in her eyes as they rolled back in her head, making the whites clearly visible.

"Stella!" I was screaming out, hoping that she might hear my familiar voice above the roar of the crowd. My horse raised her head in my direction and cried back to me, a clarion call, a high-pitched whinny that rocked through the piazza.

"Let her go!" I was shouting at the crowds. "She has won for you and now you do this to her? Let her go!"

In all this chaos I had lost Marco. And then across the piazza I saw him being dragged from his horse. Not in order to crest the wave of victory as I had been doing, but to be thrown brutally to the ground. In the Palio it is considered the greatest shame of all to come second and the men of the Porcupine contrada showed no mercy. They gathered around Marco's prone form and rained blows upon him. They kicked him and punched him and swore at him.

I screamed at them to stop, but they were like animals. No one would help him. My own contrada considered my sobs an embarrassment. Why should I care about the suffering of a Porcupine? They were our bitter rivals and Marco's beating was a symbol of my victory.

And so I could do nothing as the boy that I loved was beaten half to death by his own people, in the same piazza where they hanged my brother.

After the horrors of war, when so many had died in the fight for freedom, to see our celebration of peace degenerate into pointless brutality over something as stupid as a horse race, I was sickened and heartbroken beyond belief.

So many times I had tried to be true to my contrada, despite their ridiculous rules. For the sake of the Lupa I had kept my friendship and then later my love for Marco a secret. I had hidden my feelings because he was Porcupine and I was Wolf. Now I realised that the secrets and lies had to end. The truth would set me free.

That night, I sat Mama and Papa down at the table.

"I have something to tell you both," I said.

"Marco and I are in love. We are going to marry."

Mama began to sob. She could not look at me. She put her hands over her ears like a small child and shook her head.

"I cannot listen to this!" she shouted. "To hear that my own daughter has been allowing herself to become entangled with some filthy Istrice!"

"But I love him!" I choked back my own tears, appealing to Papa. "Please, all I want is your blessing to be with him."

Papa looked very stern. "This boy has already brought shame to his own contrada today. He is worthless and he will ruin you, Loretta. No Lupa boy will want to marry you if he knows you have been romantically involved with an Istrice! You must break it off with him immediately and we will never speak of it again."

"And what if I refuse?" I asked defiantly.

"Then," Mama spoke up, "you will no longer be our daughter."

There are moments in our lives that change who we are forever, and no matter how hard we try, we cannot return to the way things were before. I had confronted my parents and now I knew the truth. If I stayed here, I would never know happiness or peace.

"We have to leave," I told Marco that night. "We cannot be together if we stay here."

Marco's beating had left him with broken ribs. I had bandaged them, and tended to the bruises on his torso and arms, and the cuts and lacerations on his cheek. The kicks and punches were not random. They had taken it in turns, Marco explained. It was all very systematic. Each man in the Istrice contrada would step forward to take his best shot, a kick or a punch. They lined up for their go while the others cheered and bellowed. *Traitor* they called him as he lay whimpering on the ground. They said he was a dirty cheat who had thrown the race on purpose by pulling his horse up and letting me win.

It wasn't true, of course. Marco had lost the race, as jockeys do, simply because his horse was not as fast as mine. All the same, they beat him to a pulp.

Marco was so battered and bruised, he did not look like himself! One of his eyes had turned black and completely closed over. His lips were so swollen he could barely drink. I gave him a sip of water, and propped him up on the pillows that I had brought to the stables.

"Loretta, you are over-reacting," Marco said.

"Have you looked in a mirror?" I asked him in astonishment.

"It was nothing personal," Marco winced. It clearly hurt him to speak. "This is the tradition. I lost the race, I let down my contrada..."

"Marco." I shook my head. "They have done this to you! You raced your heart out for them and they repaid you like this! And what about my parents? They have told me that they will never allow us to be together. What choice do we have?"

I cast a look over at Stella who was standing in her stall. She had run her heart out for me today. I loved her so much! The thought of leaving her behind was almost more than I could bear, but I knew that what I was saying was right.

"There is a train at three o'clock tomorrow afternoon," I told Marco. "It will take us to Rome. And from there we can buy tickets on a boat to America."

"America?" Marco sat up. "You can't be serious?"

"Of course I am serious!" I pulled back from our nest in the hay and sat up. "It is the only way!"

"You are being crazy, Loretta! This will blow over, you will see..."

"If this is what they do to you when you lose a race," I said, "imagine what they will do when we tell them we want to get married. Don't you see? There is no future for us as long as the contradas control us."

Marco dropped his gaze from mine.

"So this is your solution. You want me to abandon my mother, my father, my brothers and my friends to be with you?"

"I want us to be happy and live our lives together!"

Marco shook his head. "I need time to think about this, Loretta."

"What is there to think about?" I replied. "You know that I am right and this is the only chance for us."

I clutched his hand and held it to my heart. "Meet me at the station tomorrow, Marco. If you love me, then you will be there."

There was a finality to our parting, and I lay awake that night consumed by sorrow, knowing that we were not the same as we once were, that our decisions had been made. All the same, as I stood on that platform the next day I waited in desperation for him to appear, hoping against hope. Even to the very last, as the train pulled in to the station and the passengers began to board, right up until the moment the doors were closed and the whistle sounded and we began to pull away slowly from the platform, I still believed he would come. I watched out the window, convinced I would catch a glimpse of him running around the corner, shouting out joyfully to me, sprinting to catch up with the train and make a flying leap onboard.

I sat alone in my carriage and clutched his unused ticket in my hand all the way to Rome. It was the longest and loneliest journey of my entire life, but I never looked back, and I never saw Marco again.

Storm Tamer

So many questions filled my head as Nonna finished her story, I didn't know where to begin.

"Did you ever contact Marco?" I asked. "Maybe send him a letter and let him know where you were?"

Nonna shook her head. "Marco, my brother and the war, they all became one and the same to me. Everything I had left behind in Italy caused me pain. I did not want to dwell on the past. From the moment I set foot on American soil, New York opened its heart to me and I felt free for the first time in my life.

"When I met your grandfather that day in the clubhouse and he smiled at me and helped me to pick up the broken crockery, I knew right away that he was a good man. Over the years that followed we were so happy together. I spent my days with the horses, which I loved. And then I had a baby – your father – and he grew up and got married to your mama. She was a wonderful woman, beautiful inside and out, and your father loved her very much. Then Johnny and Vincent came along and Donna and then you, Piccolina. My little one, the dearest of all to my heart."

"Nonna," I said. "I'm really sorry. I'm sorry I didn't know. After what you'd been through I never would have had anything to do with the contradas."

"It's in the past, Piccolina. It was a long time ago…"

"I don't care. I'm not going to ride for them, Nonna. Not after what they did. I'm going to tell them no."

Nonna shook her head. "That is not why I told you the story, Piccolina. I don't want you to give up the chance to ride because of what happened to me. I only wanted you to be aware of what you are getting yourself into. These men you are dealing with are capable of anything. They are not good people."

"What about the Prior? Is he a good person?"

"What do you mean?"

"I mean, do you trust him? You told me that he knew about Carlo. The Prior was the one that sent you on the mission that night. Perhaps he also sent the Blackshirts too? Maybe he wasn't on the side of the freedom fighters after all? You said the fascists treated him as one of them. Perhaps he really was a fascist all along?"

"No! Piccolina, that's not true. The Prior was helping Carlo. He did his best to protect me afterwards…"

"Or was he just trying to keep you quiet in case someone else realised what he had done?"

"It is impossible," Nonna said. "I know you do not want to believe that it is my fault, Piccolina, but I am telling you the story as it really happened. It was me. I was the one who led the Blackshirts to my brother –"

The hard rap of bare knuckles against wood made us both sit upright in our chairs. There was someone at the front door of the villa!

"It will be the Prior and the Capitano," Nonna said. "They have come to discuss strategy for your race tomorrow."

I stayed in my chair. I didn't know what to do. There was silence and then two more knocks at the door. The bang sounded ominous, this time, impatient.

"Let them in," Nonna said.

I walked to the front door with a sense of dread. After what Nonna had just told me, I was not sure what was the right thing to do any more. Should I race for the contrada or tell them that they needed to find themselves another fantino? I took a deep breath and swung the door open.

"Frannie?"

"Hi, Lola," Frannie said. "Can we come in for a moment?"

We? I looked behind him. Standing there on the doorstep in the shadows was Signor Fratelli.

"Umm, OK," I said. "I'm just in the kitchen with Nonna…"

"It is actually your nonna that I have come to see."

It was Signor Fratelli speaking. He stepped over the threshold and removed his hat.

I looked at Frannie. His expression made it clear that he was as baffled by this as I was.

"Come with me," I said.

When we entered the kitchen, Nonna had her back to us at first, busy making coffee.

"Loretta?" Signor Fratelli said her name and I saw Nonna's shoulders stiffen. She did not turn around.

"Who is it?" she said.

"You know who it is," Signor Fratelli replied.

Nonna turned around to face us. Her skin was ashen with shock. Her hand holding the coffee cup was trembling.

"It cannot be you," she whispered. "But how? Why are you here?"

"You know each other?" I asked.

There was a tense pause and then Nonna said, "We do. Although it has been a long time. Hasn't it, Marco?"

Signor Fratelli nodded. "Seventy years, Loretta. Almost to the day."

Marco. She called him Marco.

Signor Fratelli gestured to the chair. "May I sit down?" he asked.

I noticed he was holding his hat so tight, he'd screwed up the brim of it in his hands, and he was shaking too.

Nonna grunted. "At our age it does us no good to stand up."

Signor Fratelli shuffled to the table and sat down. Nonna sat opposite. Frannie and I remained where we were, not certain what to do.

"I am sorry to surprise you by turning up on the doorstep," Signor Fratelli said. "I have been wondering how best to do this, ever since Lola first arrived at the castle. I knew who she was, of course, even before she told me her name."

He smiled at Nonna. "She rides like you, Loretta. Fearless, agile, it must be in the blood."

"Is that why you have come here?" Nonna said. "To tell me that my granddaughter is a good rider?"

Signor Fratelli's smile vanished. "I know you must be angry, Loretta. I have been so anxious about this moment, about what to say. I felt like you would send me away if I tried to explain myself."

"What is there to explain?" Nonna said. "You made your position clear seventy years ago. There is no going back."

"You think I don't know that?" Signor Fratelli said. "Yes, you are right. I made my choice. It was a decision that has pained me every day for the rest of my life."

Nonna's eyes filled with tears, her voice was strained with emotion. "And you think I do not know pain, Marco? Me, who stood on that train platform right until the final boarding call and waited for you! Why didn't you come? If you loved me so much, why didn't you come?"

"Loretta, you don't understand what a force of nature you are," Signor Fratelli replied. "You are the strongest person I know. You always have been. Only you could have turned your back on your life and left everything behind. To throw yourself into the open arms of the world and let it decide your fate.

"I didn't have your courage, Loretta. I loved you more than anything, but I could not do what you did. I didn't follow you because I was afraid to leave my old life behind. It was all I knew and I was too cowardly to let it go."

"But we would have been together!" Nonna said. "There was nothing to be afraid of!"

"For you, maybe, but I was not ready to cut the ties," Signor Fratelli said. "It was only after you were gone, Loretta, that I realised I could be brave too, in my own small way. I confronted the Prior of the Porcupines and told him I was no longer a part of the contrada. Then I struck out on my own and began to breed and train Palio horses for myself. I used all the skills I had learnt from my time with you, the way you treated your horses and trained them. I never had an eye for a horse like you did, but I was skilled in my own way and soon I had a reputation for producing the best Palio horses in Italy. All the contradas began to come to me. I belonged to no contrada, but they needed me and there was a freedom in that, of sorts at least."

Signor Fratelli was still anxiously clutching his hat. "I tried to find you, Loretta. But I had no idea where you were. I didn't even know for sure whether you had made it to New York. If only you had written to me, just one letter saying where you were."

"What for?" Nonna said. "You made your choice, Marco. I wasn't going to try and convince you to come after me."

"No." Signor Fratelli shook his head. "That's not why I tried to find you. I loved you still, but I never expected you to take me back. I was trying to find you for a different reason. To tell you what I had found out, because you needed to know the truth."

"What are you talking about?" Nonna said.

Signor Fratelli hesitated. "Loretta, I need to tell you about Carlo, about what really happened the night that his camp was seized by the Blackshirts."

Nonna stiffened. "I know what happened that night."

"No, you don't," Signor Fratelli said. "Neither did I, not until much later, almost two years after you had left Siena…

"They said the war was over, but there was no real peace in Italy yet. The civil war meant ongoing trials and recriminations as the fascists, who had done terrible things, were hunted out and brought to justice.

"One day, I was exercising one of the horses

when I came across a group of men hiding out in the woods. They were in a bad way, they looked as if they had been living rough for some time. It was clear to me that they were Blackshirts on the run from the authorities. I had seen them but they had not seen me, so I rode back as fast as I could and went to the police. The men were arrested and taken in for questioning.

"I was not there for the interrogation myself. The rest of the story I learnt in a bar that evening when I shared a drink with the chief of police. He told me that the men were indeed Blackshirts, and that they had confessed to several acts against the freedom fighters, including the attack on your brother's camp in the woods.

"I don't know why I had the presence of mind to ask the chief of police, but as we sat with our wine, talking about what had happened in the woods the night Carlo had been captured, I had one very important question for him.

"'How did the Blackshirts find the freedom fighters' camp? Did someone lead them there?'

"The police chief sucked hard on his cigarette.

'Not a person at all,' he said. 'It was a dog who showed them the way. The patrol came across him, a scruffy brown thing, lost in the woods. And what do you think the foolish beast did? With a little bit of coaxing, he led the Blackshirts right where they wanted to go.'

"The chief of police shook his head, 'Poor dumb mutt. Man's best friend indeed! His loyalty to his master was what did them in.'"

Nonna's eyes widened. "Ludo?"

Signor Fratelli nodded. "That was why I tried to find you, Loretta. It wasn't you who led the Blackshirts to Carlo at all. It was the dog."

Signor Fratelli pushed his chair back and stood up from the table.

"Carlo's death was a tragedy, Loretta, but it was not your fault. There is no blood on your hands. Now at last you know the truth."

Signor Fratelli readied himself to leave and beckoned to Frannie, who stood up with him and they began to walk towards the door.

"Wait!" Nonna said.

Signor Fratelli turned around.

"There is coffee," Nonna said. "A fresh pot and Lola has made biscotti. They are very nice, not as good as mine, maybe, but she is learning. Please? Stay a while?"

Signor Fratelli took his hat off again and walked back to the table.

"I should like that very much," he said.

Signor Fratelli and Frannie stayed for dinner in the end. Nonna prepared wonderful gnocchi and we ate green salad from the garden and Frannie and I sat at the table and listened as our grandparents told us endless stories of their childhood. Not the sad stories, but the happy ones now. Tales about stealing fruit from the neighbourhood's apricot tree, and swimming horses in the lagoon, and bow and arrow fights on horseback.

At last, it was almost eleven at night and Signor Fratelli and my nonna bid each other goodnight.

I walked with Frannie to the end of the driveway, and we talked about the Palio. I had made up my mind now, I would race.

"The next time I see you," I told him, "you will be

my deadly enemy."

He laughed. "That is what the contrada might say, but you and I do not belong to them, do we?"

"No," I agreed. "We don't."

"You know Umberto and Leonardo were selected too?" Frannie said. "We will all be on the track tomorrow, so perhaps the Contrada of the Wolf will have friends for once, as well as foes."

"I'll need them," I said. "I'm terrified."

"Don't be," Frannie told me. "You are ready for this. Nico is too. He is in fine form. He ate a good dinner tonight before they took him away."

"Took him away?" I said.

"It is tradition," Frannie said. "The night before the Palio, the chosen one must sleep in the stall beneath the contrada."

"When did they take him?"

"Just before we left to come to you," Frannie said.

"But Nico will hate that! He'll be all alone down there!"

I turned away and headed back up the driveway to the villa.

"Where are you going?" Frannie called after me.

"I have to go tell Nonna," I said, "I'm going to the contrada to see Nico."

"They'll never let you in," Frannie said. "Nobody can see the horse on the night before the race."

"I don't care!" I shouted back to him. "I have to try!"

Back at the villa I burst inside and hurried up the stairs. "Nonna! I just found out the contrada have taken Nico! I have to go and…"

"Lola! I am in here…"

Nonna was in her bedroom.

"I need you to get something for me, Piccolina," she said. "It is underneath the bed and I have tried but my bones are too stiff to bend down that low."

"What is it?" I asked.

"There should be a suitcase under there," Nonna said. "A brown leather one with gold initials on the front."

I lay down on my belly and looked under the bed. A thick layer of dust covered the floorboards, and I had to suppress a sneeze.

"I can see the case," I said. "It's right at the back by the wall."

"There should be a handle," Nonna said. "Can

you drag it out?"

"Urghh." I stretched my arm as far as I could, flattening my chest to the floor. "Got it!"

I dragged the case out and put it up on the bed, wiping the dust from the top with my hand.

"Open it."

I did as she asked, clicking the lock on the case and opened the lid.

Inside were racing silks, handmade from beautiful, heavy satin. The trousers were black and white check and the top half the same, with stripes of brilliant orange.

"Take them out. They should be your size," Nonna said. "They fitted me once."

I held the racing silks up against me and looked at my reflection in the mirror. It was really happening. I was going to ride the Palio.

"You will need something else," Nonna said. "It is not enough to have the silks, you must also have your nickname."

"Can't I just use yours?" I asked. "Can't I be *Scavezzecolla?*"

"Ah!" Nonna grinned. "There was only one

273

Daredevil, and that was me! No, Piccolina, you must be your own name. You shall be *Tempesta*."

I frowned. "What does that mean, *Tempesta*?"

"It means that of all the fantinos you alone are a storm tamer," my nonna said. "You are the girl who can ride the wind."

Midnight in the Via di Vallerozzi

It was almost midnight when I reached the Via di Vallerozzi. I hurried as fast as I dared in the dark on the steep, cobbled streets, all the time growing more and more sick with worry about Nico. How could they just take him like that? All his life he'd had the company of the other horses at Signor Fratelli's stables. How must he have felt when he was handed over to complete strangers, taken to the subterranean stalls beneath the contrada and left there all alone in the darkness! He must be terrified! I didn't care about the stupid Lupa traditions – I had to go to him.

At the entrance to the Contrada of the Wolf I raised

my eyes to the bell tower above and felt the knot in my belly tighten. Taking a deep breath, I stepped up to the door and knocked, rapping four times then four again, this was the code of the contrada that Nonna had given to me.

"Nonna," I had said to her. "It's been seventy years since you entered the doors. Don't you think they would have changed the code?"

Nonna had laughed. "Piccolina, you must have learnt by now that nothing ever changes in Siena!"

There was a creak of ancient hinges as the massive oak door opened and the guardsman poked his head out.

"Hello, signor…"

"No tourists, Americano! Not on the night before the Palio."

"I'm not a tourist! I'm Lola. Lola Campione."

I'm sure the guardsman would have thrown me out if the Capitano hadn't come when he did. As he led me through the maze of corridors. There was a sense of urgency to his stride so that I had to scurry behind him to keep up.

When he pulled down hard on the two swords I

watched in astonishment as the wolf's head split in two to reveal the dark stairwell on the other side.

"You must go alone from here. I need to return to my meeting."

I descended the stairs, clutching at the walls in the darkness, until I reached the narrow underground passage that led to Nico's stall.

"Hello?" My voice echoed in the darkened corridor. Ahead of me there was a door, with bars on the window. I could hear the restless stamping of hooves on soft straw.

"Nico?"

The stupid bolt was stuck! I thought I would break my fingers trying to force it open and in the end I had to shove it with all my strength so that it came loose. Then I ran to him, flinging my arms around his golden neck, burying my face deep in the coarse strands of his flaxen mane.

"Of course I came," I whispered. "You didn't think I would leave you here alone, did you? I'll always come for you, Nico, no matter what."

I have always talked to horses. In the stables at Aqueduct I would chat away to Snickers and Sonic as

I mucked out their boxes and groomed them. But that night, when I was talking to Nico, it was different. It was like he understood me, like he was really listening, the way he would swivel his ears back and forth when I talked about winning the race, the way he looked at me with his deep, soulful brown eyes, like this meant every bit as much to him as it did to me.

"Tomorrow," I told him, "you and me, we're going to go out there and prove it to them and win this crazy bareback race in front of all of Italy and everyone in the piazza and when we cross the line together we'll be heroes and the whole contrada's going to remember you for ever…"

We talked for hours that night. Well, I talked and Nico listened, I suppose. I told him stories about my life in New York, about walking to school in winter, scared that I was going to slip on black ice on the footpath, and eating warm bagels with pastrami from Sheinken's delicatessen.

I told Nico the whole story that night about Jake Mayo. I knew that when I got home, things would be different between us. I saw Jake for what he really was now and I felt sorry for him. His entire universe was the school playground, where he could be a big man and act like he was the king. But there was a bigger world, one where real things were important, and that was the one I lived in now. Frannie, Umberto, Leonardo and Antonia had become my friends, not because of what shoes I wore to school, or whether I was cool or not. It no longer mattered to me what Jake thought of me, or whether he tried to goad me by making whinnying noises when I walked by.

"He's just a dumb kid," I told Nico. And I wasn't a kid any more. I was a fantino.

I told Nico all about my dad too, about how overprotective he was.

"He would never let me ride in the Palio if he was here," I said. "He won't even let me ride track back home."

Nico shook his mane.

"I know!" I said. "Silly, right? Plus he has this thing about me 'getting educated'." I stroked Nico's muzzle.

"He's like that because of my mom. She had cancer, and she died when I was little, so I don't remember what it was like when she was around, except sometimes I'll get flashes of memory, like words she used to say, or the way she brushed my hair. Anyway, Dad says if Mom was alive she would have been proud of how good I am at school and she would have wanted me to go to university, like she never had the chance to do, even though she was real smart. It's because of her that he's so hot under the collar about it. He wants me to be some fancy pants doctor or something…"

I looked at Nico, expecting him to take my side, but he had these deep creases above his brown eyes, like he was frowning with concern.

"Not you too!" I groaned. "OK, OK. How about a compromise? Maybe I could go to medical school during the day and ride trackwork in the mornings? I can do both, right?"

I liked this new solution.

"And when I'm a famous doctor, I'm going to buy Dad and Nonna a new house, and it will have my own room in it so I won't have to share with Donna any more."

It was getting late, probably around three a.m., but it was hard to tell. There was a small window in the stall with steel bars like a prison cell to look out into the enclosed courtyard. We were beneath the contrada's headquarters, sunken down a level from the street, so even when I peered out through the bars, I couldn't see anything really except the red-brick basement walls of the contrada. I turned to look at Nico. He was sleeping. His eyes were closed anyway, even though he was still standing up, but then horses often slept that way. I lay down on the straw on the floor of the stall, thinking I might close my eyes just for a moment.

At first, I thought I must be imagining the noise in the courtyard. I had looked out the window just a moment ago and I was certain there was nothing there. It was a scratching, faint at first and then louder, more insistent. Then, another noise that made me almost jump out of my skin. A low, deep growl.

I could feel the blood pounding through my veins, my heart racing. I sat up in the straw. The growl reverberated through me, almost as if it was coming not from outside the bars, but from in me: this primal, animal noise.

I listened as the growl grew louder outside in the courtyard. I was afraid to move, but I knew I had to look. I summoned up the nerve and got to my feet and walked towards the window. I couldn't see anything out there.

I leant closer, putting my face right up against the bars.

That was when the wolf leapt. She thrust herself up on her hind legs, paws spread-eagled on the walls on either side of the window, jaws open and teeth bared, right up against the iron bars.

I screamed and threw myself backwards, scrambling on all fours on the straw, pressing myself against the door of the stall, trying to get away.

The wolf stared at me, eyes as cold as steel. "Tempesta, daughter of the She-Wolf. Bravest of all seventeen. You know you do not need to fear me."

I had my back pinned against the door, I could feel my heart thumping in my chest. And then I saw Nico.

He stood with his ears pricked forward, utterly calm in the presence of this vicious predator.

So the creature was telling the truth. There was no need to be afraid. I took a deep breath to calm myself and walked back to her. Up close, the bars still separated us, but I could smell her meaty breath and see the thick, glassy saliva as it dripped

282

from her porcelain fangs.

"Good. You understand," she said with a low growl. "The time is nearly upon us, Tempesta. I have come to prepare you."

"For the race?"

The wolf snarled, her temper flashing hot. "The Palio is more than a race. It is life and death!"

Then, as quickly as she had become angry, she was calm once more. "They say the Lupa has no friends. This is not true. You will have three of them, trust them with your life, Tempesta."

Growling softly she said, "You will have enemies too. There are traitors in the house of Lupa. They think you are a cub. Not ready for the battle. But they don't know you like I do, Lola Campione. I know the fighter you have inside you..."

The wolf's grey eyes suddenly swept to the door. Her ears flattened as if she had heard something that displeased her. Then, without a word, she leapt down from the window and was gone. I was looking for her, peering out into the darkness, when I felt a hand grasp me on my shoulder. "Lola!"

Suddenly I wasn't standing at the window any

more. I was lying on the straw on the floor of Nico's stall. The dawn light was pouring in through the steel bars of the window and the Capitano was at my side, shaking me gently awake.

"Where did the wolf go?" I sat up, rubbing my eyes.

"Wolf?" The Capitano looked confused.

"She was here…" I stopped myself, realising how crazy I sounded. "I'm sorry, I must have been dreaming…"

The Capitano frowned. "You need to go home, Lola," he said. "The grooms will be here soon to prepare Nico for the blessing, and you should be ready too."

"What's the blessing?"

"A sacred ritual," the Capitano replied. "Every fantino and their horse must be blessed before the race."

"But how will I know what I'm supposed to do?"

The Capitano smiled at me. "Ask your grandmother to tell you," he said. "I am sure she will remember. After all, she has done it before."

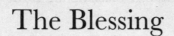

The Blessing

The Pope came to New York once and he held mass at Aqueduct. This was before I was born, but I know all about what happened because Nonna Loretta told me the story. She said there were more people at Aqueduct that day than for any horse race, even the famous ones with Secretariat. The Pope arrived in a helicopter and everyone cheered him and he made a speech and blessed everyone. After that, Nonna said it didn't matter that we never went to church on Sundays because Aqueduct was holy ground.

As I walked down the Via di Vallerozzi that afternoon, for the first time I regretted my lack of religious education. I had no idea how to act in church, kneeling down and crossing your chest and that sort of thing. And now here I was about to receive a sacred blessing in front of the whole contrada.

Nonna had explained what I had to do, but all the same I was worried that I would miss my cue or mess it up.

As we neared the buildings of the Lupa it looked like a big Italian wedding was taking place. There were families on the doorstep of the church, all dressed in their best clothes, happy and laughing. Banners in the colour of our contrada had been strung across the Via di Vallerozzi and on the steps the Capitano was greeting everyone with a broad smile, shaking hands and kissing cheeks.

Nonna tightened her grip on my arm and I wasn't sure if she was trying to steady herself, or if she sensed my nerves and was trying to reassure me that it would all be OK. Then her hand clung to me even more and I felt her pull me back.

"I just need a moment, Lola," she said.

I turned and saw the look on her face, and I realised she was afraid too.

"It's OK, Nonna," I whispered. "I'm here with you."

"You're a good girl, Lola." Nonna gave my hand a squeeze and I felt how frail she was, her tiny hands like sparrow claws, skin as thin as paper. We began to walk again as the bells began chiming out, calling everyone inside.

The Capitano stayed on the stairs, encouraging everyone to enter and take their seats. When he saw me and Nonna he walked over to greet us, kissing Nonna Loretta solemnly on both cheeks. Then he placed a hand on my shoulder. "Lola, you are ready to be blessed?"

I nodded.

The Capitano took my grandmother's arm. "I have a seat for you at the front, Loretta," he said. "Come with me." He led her inside and I was about to follow but he shook his head.

"You wait here. We will come for you when we are ready to begin."

I watched as the people went inside and took their seats. It was a tight squeeze getting everyone into the pews. Eventually, I was the only one left outside.

I stepped up to the door and peeked in. It was like the Sistine Chapel in there with high domed ceilings covered in elaborate paintings of cherubs and angels in shades of peach and duck-egg blue trimmed with gold. The walls were painted with frescos of the Virgin Mary, in dark colours edged with more gold.

As the organ music struck up the chatter in the church stopped and the Capitano strode out purposefully to me.

"It is time," he said. "Come, Lola."

Inside, I heard the doors clank shut behind me, and then the organ really started up, playing my theme music. I began to walk up the aisle slowly one step and then the next, like a bride to the Wedding March. My heart was hammering in my chest and I could hardly breathe. When I reached the altar I cast a sneaky glance at Nonna in the front row and she nodded to me as if to say, "You're doing fine". Then the curtains in front of me parted and the priest appeared.

Dressed in long robes and carrying a golden flask he stepped up to the altar and began shuffling gold ornaments around. Then he turned to face the crowd and in a dramatic gesture he raised his hand above me, and reached out and touched his palm to my forehead. I dropped to my knees and knelt before the priest.

The organ stopped. There was a spooky silence and then, from outside the church came the shouting. There were men yelling out to each other and the Capitano's voice loudest of all, crying, "Hold him! Ho! There!"

Suddenly the church doors swung wide open and Nico was standing there. A murmur ran through the pews at the sight of him, his chestnut coat shining in the sunlight, even brighter than the polished gold of the church altar.

The men were struggling to get him inside, but Nico was refusing to move. He had his ears flat back in fear and you could see the whites of his eyes rolling in his head as he fought them. They crowded in on all sides, trying to urge him forward, but Nico resisted, stamping his hooves and shaking his mane in defiance.

The Capitano shouted something in Italian and the men linked arms to make a human chain, circling around behind Nico, using their weight against his rump to make him step forward.

Blowing hard through his nostrils, Nico gave a loud snort and then with an almighty lunge he leapt inside the church! There were shrieks from the people in the pews as he surged past them and his hooves clattered against the tiled floor of the aisle. He trotted with his knees high, dragging his handlers on ropes on either side of him. They held on as if he were a hot air balloon and they were anchoring him, until he came to a stop beside me right in front of the altar.

Poor Nico! He was wet with sweat, his flanks heaving with anxiety. I could see by the look in his eyes that he was terrified.

I wanted to tell him I felt the same way, that neither of us should have been in this place. I mean, me, a twelve-year-old kid from Ozone Park, and him a horse, being blessed in front of God and everyone when neither of us had even been to church before in our lives!

The priest seemed to know that Nico was ready to blow up. He was trying to get the ceremony over and done with, chanting in double-quick time. "Oh, God, defend your servant, Lola Campione, through the dangers of the coming race." He shook some more water on me and I felt this sense of relief that we were nearly done. I was about to rise to my feet when I smelt something. Rising above the waft of incense and altar candles came a dark stink. I looked behind me in horror to see Nico raise his tail and with a *plop-plop-plop* a pile of dung dropped to the middle of the aisle on the church floor.

"Nooo," I groaned in embarrassment.

"Lu-Lu-Lupa! Lu-Lu-Lupa!!"

But the crowd were cheering!

"It is a good omen!" The priest was beaming with delight at the pile of muck. He stepped forward and stuck his shoe right in there, squishing down deep into it. "I stand in the excrement to bring even more good luck!" he cried.

I looked at Nonna, like I hadn't realised until that moment just how much crazy there was in the room. She gave me a shrug, as if to say, "What did I tell you?"

The priest raised his hands in the air and exhorted

to me and Nico, "Go, our champions and return as winners!"

"Lu-Lu-Lupa!" The people leapt up and rushed at us, overwhelming poor Nico!

There was a gasp as he reared and thrashed the air with his hooves, and the crowd scattered momentarily, but as soon as he had all four feet on the ground they surged on him again!

"Nico!" He was terrified. "Leave him alone!" I couldn't reach him. I was being carried away, lifted off my feet like a ragdoll, caught up by the crowd.

They took me out to the Via di Vallerozzi and I was placed on the back of a horse. Not Nico, but a plain brown pony, thick-boned and stocky.

Nonna had told me this would happen because the fantino doesn't ride their racehorse to the piazza. Only when I reached the square and the race was ready to begin would I be reunited with Nico.

They led me along through the streets as if I was a small child being given a pony ride. All the way there was chanting and singing and flag-waving. I kept looking for Nico and for Nonna, but even if I had been able to see them I could never have reached them. There were hundreds of supporters, crushing in around me.

As we got closer to the square, we merged with other contradas, also with fantinos mounted on ponies. We were like streams joining together to become a river, forming one great rushing torrent as we reached the piazza.

I had never seen so many people in one place. There were more than at Aqueduct on the day the Pope came in his helicopter. All around the buildings they had built grandstands and these were filled up so that the people seemed to be stacked on top of one another all the way to the balconies above, and in the middle of the piazza thousands and thousands of spectators were crammed behind the barriers.

They had been standing there for hours already, baking in the hot sun and watching the parades. Men in those *Romeo and Juliet* costumes were trooping about, waving the flags as if they were swords, bowing and leaping while others banged the marching drums slung at their hips.

As each contrada paraded past, the crowd would start up with their chants. "Lu-Lu-Lupa!" If a rival went past they would shout abuse at them. A three-year-old perched on his father's shoulder waved his flag and shouted "*Puzza!*" at the Giraffe contrada. It meant "Giraffes! You stink!"

Everywhere in the crowd, the tension threatened to bubble over into violence and I thought of Marco, dragged from his horse and beaten and kicked for coming second. Only now that I was here and it was too late, did I finally realise the truth of the Palio.

This was not just a race, this was an ancient feud. I wasn't a jockey. I was the champion of my people, a gladiator being sent into battle. And for a gladiator, there were only two options. Victory or death.

"Lola!"

It was the Capitano. He was dressed in a new costume, not his long flowing robes that he had worn in the church, but a medieval-looking skirt and tights and puffy sleeves like the other men. He was leading Nico to me.

"It is time," he said.

I slid down off the back of the brown pony and vaulted up onto Nico's back.

"Listen to me, Lola, this is important," the

Capitano said. "Now the race is upon us, the other fantinos will try to do deals with you. They will make you offers, tell you that you will never win anyway and that they will offer you money if you will take their side and help them to victory!"

Beneath me, Nico had started to skip anxiously, as if the soil under his hooves was a furnace and he could not bear to stand still.

"I know, Capitano," I said. "I've been told about it."

"Ah," the Capitano said. "So you understand that sometimes it is in the best interest of the contrada to stand back and let another take the glory?"

I felt myself stiffen.

"What?"

"Lola," the Capitano leant close to me and hissed in a low whisper, "here is the thing. You have drawn a bad position. Very bad. You are on the outside of the track. The Contrada of the Dragon have the mighty Primo, the greatest stallion the Palio has ever known. And they have the *Assassino* riding for them! He has won this race thirteen times. You know you cannot beat him."

"Are you saying you want me to lose on purpose?" I said. "Because I won't do that."

"Do you really think you can win?" the Capitano snarled. "You are a cub! Not ready for the battle!"

A cub. Not ready for the battle! The words the wolf had spoken to me last night.

"Capitano!"

I heard the voice of the Prior and looked up to see the old man pushing through the crowd to reach us. He had my nonna with him, keeping his arm protectively around her. I wasn't sure if he had heard all of our conversation, but by the look of fury on his face I was guessing he'd heard most of it.

"For five years now," the Prior said, "ever since you have been in charge of the Palio, the Lupa have lost the race. And always the excuses. You say we have had bad horses and terrible fantinos. Now we've drawn the outside track. We cannot win. And so you tell this child to lose on purpose?"

The Capitano spluttered, "I was trying to make us some money. The Contrada of the Dragon have agreed my terms."

"You negotiated a deal without my consent?" the Prior said.

"I did what is best for the contrada," the Capitano said. "We should ally ourselves with the Dragon."

"And lose the race before it is run?" The Prior shook his head. "This is not the way of the Lupa. I will not allow it."

"You cannot stop me. The Capitano has ultimate power to advise the fantino. You should not even be here!"

"You are right, of course," the Prior said. "You are still the Capitano and if you choose to invoke the laws of the Palio we must leave."

The Capitano looked smug until the Prior added, "But if you do, I will take the decision right here and now in front of everyone to strip you of your role and I will appoint Loretta Campione as the new Capitano."

The Capitano's face fell. "You are not serious."

"I am," the Prior replied. "Now step out of the way and let the signora talk to her granddaughter because, of the two of you standing here right now, she is the only one who knows how to win a Palio."

There was a stony silence and the two men stared hard at each other. Then the Capitano reluctantly stepped back. "It makes no difference," he said. "The race is lost anyway."

The Prior held my nonna's hand to steady her as she came forward until she was right beside Nico's shoulder.

"Are you all right, Piccolina?" she asked.

"I'm OK, Nonna."

"Good girl!" Nonna said. "Now, ignore the Capitano. Forget everything he said to you because he is a fool. A rider can still win, even if they have drawn a position right at the outside of the track. You just need to ride the perfect race, and you will do that because you are my granddaughter."

I smiled at this and Nonna grunted with satisfaction. "Right. Here is how you will ride. You see the first corner? I have told you already that it is the most treacherous one on the course. The other riders will shove you and kick you, force you out to the edge of the track, send you crashing into the wall. You must ride a tight line, Piccolina, do not let them push you out.

"Once you are clear of the first turn, do not take the lead. You must hold Nico back now, pull him back if you need to and wait to make your move."

"How far back?"

"You keep him right at the rear until the very last lap."

"Right at the rear? You mean behind everyone?"

Nonna nodded. "Let them tire their horses out. Keep Nico in range, and wait. Hold him until the very last lap, then you make your move."

She paused and looked around, as if she was worried about being overheard, then she leant close to me. "Piccolina, do not draw attention to yourself, but if you look behind me you will see a fantino on a big grey horse. He wears purple, green and yellow, the colours of the Dragon. Do you see him?"

I nodded. "Yes."

"That is *Assassino*, the Assassin. He will stop at nothing to beat you. Do not let your guard down for a moment. When you make your challenge at the end of the race, the Assassin will be right up there at the front waiting for you. His horse, Primo, he is fast, very fast. But your Nico is faster –"

The bells sounded, their clamour the signal for everyone except the fantinos and their mounts to clear the track.

Nonna reached up and grasped my hand one last time. "Good luck, Piccolina. May fortune favour you. Ride the wind!"

The time had come. We were about to race.

The Palio

When my dad was still a jockey, I remember watching him in the changing rooms at Aqueduct as he put on his boots. He was about to race and yet he looked totally calm, humming away to himself as he threaded the laces.

"Don't you feel scared?" I asked him.

"Of course I do, Lola," Dad said. "You always get nerves before a race. Any jockey who says they don't, they're either a liar or a fool."

"Why are they fools?"

"Because a rider needs the fear, that's what gets the adrenaline pumping. You get that shot of adrenaline and suddenly: POW! Your brain goes into overdrive. Your reactions speed up, and it's like you can see everything around you as if the whole world is in slow motion and you're going at the speed of light."

"So being afraid is good?"

Dad gave his laces a jerk. "A little bit of the fear is very good. But too much? No. Then you tip over the edge in the other direction. You panic and make the wrong move, you second-guess yourself. You take crazy risks."

"How will I know if I have the right amount of the fear in me?"

"You'll never know until the time comes, Lola," he said. "That's how life works. It isn't until we're put to the test that we know if we've got the stuff inside of us."

As the bells chimed out and the Prior ushered my nonna from the track, I looked out over the crowded piazza and I felt the fear rip through me like electricity.

This was no wild-ride-at-an-amusement-park fear, that sense of excitement you get freewheeling down a hill on your bike with your feet in mid-air off the pedals. My fear disabled me. I felt my legs turn to jelly and I was struck with the sudden, desperate urge to pee.

Nico felt my nerves. He started to act crazy, crab-stepping his way down the track, past the crowds in the piazza to the steps of the town hall, in an agitated, sideways jog, swinging his hindquarters, tail swishing, a foam of white sweat forming on his neck.

"Easy Nico." I tried to calm him with a stroke on the neck but my hands were shaking too much. The bell sounded again but the other fantinos ignored it and continued their parading around the piazza with their chests puffed out and chins held high as if they had already won the race, riding glory laps and raising their hands to high-five the crowd as they breezed past the stands. Behind the barriers the capitanos were bellowing instructions at them, but their voices were drowned out by the deafening roar of the crowds. Everywhere you looked everything was a haze of heat and noise, madness and chaos. My arms were killing me from trying to hold onto Nico. He had his ears flat back and every time another horse came near him he acted like a stallion, giving these little squeals, all tensed up with his neck arched, and his tail swishing so vigorously it was like a jet propeller behind him. He was ready to explode.

"Lola!" It was Frannie, waving to me. He had taken his position behind the rope right by the inside of the track. He gave me the thumbs up as if to ask if I was OK and all I could do was nod. I wasn't OK at all. I was pretty sure I was about to throw up. On either side of me at the rope the fantinos began to shove their way into position. I was hyperventilating, unable to breathe. My heart was pounding like I was going to have a heart attack.

Then the rope pulled taut, a single thread on which everything depended, and in that instant everything changed. In a flash my sickness was gone and I felt my blood surge, filling my veins with steel. The fear that had sapped me and turned me to jelly just moments before had mutated. Now it transformed into pure adrenaline, making my heart beat at double-speed, turning the blur around me into sharp focus. The sand of the piazza stretched ahead of me, shimmering like pure gold, and I felt Nico gather himself up, his hindquarters set to propel us like rocket thrusters. We were ready for this. I had the stuff.

Nico broke so fast he almost sprang across the rope as it was still falling, and immediately I began to pump my arms and legs to drive him on.

"Go!" I leant forward and urged him on. "Go, Nico!"

We were right in amongst the pack and all around me there were fantinos driving and pushing and jostling for position. Nonna had told me I would need to hold my line into the corner, but it was only now that I realised how impossible this was, as all the riders surged at once for the same gap.

I was stuck on the outside of the fantino for the Eagle contrada and he kept shoving me further and further out until I had nowhere to go. I gave a squeal as my leg was crushed hard against the mattresses, leaving me no choice but to pull Nico up hard and let the Eagle pass.

Outwitted at the first turn! We had completely lost our advantage and had been driven to the back of the pack. *Pull yourself together, don't get rattled, you can come back from this,* I told myself. Even though we were right at the back of the field now, Nico felt good. He was running strong, his breath coming in excited, raspy snorts.

I could see Umberto up ahead, trailing second-to-last and dropping further behind with each stride. He'd been hoping for the ride on Dante, but after the trial races the stallion had been handed to one of the famous fantinos and Umberto had no choice but to take the ride for the Snail contrada who had put him on a sluggish dark bay named Benita. The mare was already flagging. As I pulled up alongside them Umberto raised a hand and gave me a high-five.

"This will not be my day," he shouted, "but it could be yours, Lola, good luck! Ride to win, kid!"

Passing Umberto's horse seemed to give Nico the boost he needed. He was in the race now and stretching out to gain on the others and his strides chewed up the ground as I passed by the next two riders.

I was right up alongside the Giraffe fantino, keeping a wary eye on him, when I heard a cry on the other side of me.

"Lola! Look out!" I turned just in time to see the fantino from the Unicorn contrada lining me up for a brutal shoulder charge that would have caught me completely off-guard.

Leonardo swept in between us and before the

Unicorn could swing his whip Leonardo had moved to block him, as if duelling with a sword.

"Leonardo!" I was about to swerve to go to his aid but Leonardo shook his head.

"Keep going!" Leonardo shouted. "You ride on. I got this. Go! Go!"

I did as he said and bent down low over Nico's neck, urging him on. We were flying now, and as we passed the town hall the screams of the crowd around us were deafening. One lap down, two laps to go. I was in the middle of the field now and at the first turn I kept my line and rode on and out the other side. We had reached the straight and I felt Nico pulling like a train, desperate to be let go.

"No!" I fought to keep him back. "It's too soon. Not yet, not yet…"

Nico was reefing at the reins, determined to be let free. I gave him his head just a little, enough so that he could reach the pack in front of us. There were three horses racing abreast and we tucked in behind them. Being boxed in like this gave my arms a rest, as I assessed the field.

The lack of stamina was beginning to show for

some. I saw the Panther, the Owl and the Eagle – the early leaders, flagging. They had run the tank dry just like Nonna said they would, But Nico was still running strong and when I saw the hole open up by the railing I knew that this was it. Our time had come.

"OK, Nico, let's go!"

Nico gave a snort of excitement and I felt him unleash the speed that he had been holding back all this time. All I had to do was cluck him on and he flew through the gap between the horses in front of us. We were so quick the fantinos didn't have a chance to lay a hand on us. In only two strides we were out and in the clear and bearing down on the leaders. There were just two riders ahead of us, Frannie on his big bay, Roccia, and the Assassin on Primo.

As we came into the third lap Nico's strides were no longer fluid, I could feel the effort in them. This was the moment my nonna had told me about, when a truly great horse finds himself at the end of his run and must dig down deep and find something more inside himself.

"You can do it, Nico," I urged him. "It's in you, I know it is."

Nico heard me and I'm sure he understood. He

gathered his limbs underneath him and he sprinted. I felt him stretch out low to the ground and as I urged him and called to him he responded with every muscle and fibre until we were flying.

When we ran up alongside Frannie, his horse tried his best to keep stride with us, but it was futile. Nico was too much for Roccia. We were a neck ahead and then a length and then two. I looked back over my shoulder for a moment and I saw the look of disappointment on Frannie's face, but he nodded his head bravely to me. "It's yours this time, Lola," he called out. "Go!"

We were halfway around the third lap now and only the Assassin and Primo stood between us and victory. Ahead of us I could see Primo's mighty grey rump, rising and falling with every stride, and I realised just how enormous the grey horse really was. He was a monster! Seventeen hands and musclebound, with the thick neck of a stallion and powerful haunches. So much bigger than Nico, and yet we were gaining on him.

Nico wasn't daunted by this big grey beast. Unflinching and unbowed, he began to inch forward, fighting stride for stride to take the lead from Primo.

For a moment the two horses were neck and neck and then Nico just managed to get his nose out in front and then his neck. He had beaten Primo! We had taken the lead! There was no one else ahead of us now. I could see the finish line. We were going to win and Primo, the unbeatable, incredible Primo, was about to lose.

And then from out of nowhere, I felt this blow, like a truck had hit us. Later, in the hospital, Frannie, who witnessed everything, would tell me that this was the moment when the Assassin rammed Primo right into Nico's hindquarters.

"It was the most dangerous thing I have ever seen," Frannie told me. "He risked his own horse's life to take you down. He was willing to die, I think, as long as it meant you didn't win."

There was the moment of impact as Primo hit us, and then, even worse, the sickening feeling as we plummeted downwards in slow motion, Nico struggling to regain his footing in the soft, deep sand by the mattress barrier. I did the only thing I could, I grabbed frantically at the reins trying to help him rebalance. For a second it seemed certain that we were going down in a tangle of limbs and then I felt Nico plant both forelegs to give a little buck with his hindquarters, correcting his stride, and then we were up and galloping once more and I could hear the crowd right beside us roar with joy.

"Lupa! Lupa! Lupa!"

The line was so close now, but I knew the fight between us was not over. The Assassin was powering up beside us again. He had his whip raised and as he drew up next to us he began to lash with it, trying to hit out at Nico.

"Leave him alone!" I was screaming at him, but he kept raining blow after blow. When he struck Nico's shoulder there was blood where the whip had cut the flesh and when I saw it, I guess that was when I lost it.

I no longer cared about winning the race. All I wanted was to protect my horse.

"Over all these years I've seen a lot in the Palio," Frannie told me, "but never before a fantino actually throw themselves from a galloping horse to attack another rider."

I didn't really mean to jump. I only tried to shove the Assassin, to get him away from Nico, but as my hands grabbed his silks, a chasm opened up between our horses and I refused to let him go, dragging him down with me as I plummeted into the void.

When I landed on the dirt, it was reflexes that made me cradle my head just in time as the horses right behind me came over the top of us. Through the slits of my fingers I saw the hooves pass a whisker above me. Then I heard the roar of the crowd and I knew the race was done and that they were coming for me. Coming to punish me for what I had done.

I had been in the lead when I threw myself like a lunatic at the Assassin. If I had only ignored his futile, hateful attack on Nico then I would have made it there ahead of him. Instead, in a moment of madness trying to protect Nico, I had taken the entire Wolf contrada down with me. I had thrown myself from the winning horse with just metres of the race left to run, just a few short strides from the finish line.

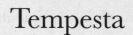

Tempesta

The hospital of Saint Maria is an ancient stone building surrounded by green gardens. Inside, the rooms are modern, though, clean and bright, and the nurses in their crisp white uniforms are lovely the way they fuss over you and smile when you say "*grazie*".

I visited Frannie there every day until they discharged him. I felt so guilty, even though he insisted it wasn't my fault. "I'm the one who should be apologising to you. I rode straight over the top of you. It's lucky I didn't kill you."

When I threw myself from Nico's back Frannie was right behind us. His horse vaulted over me and caught a leg as he landed and Frannie was somersaulted into the path of his own mount.

"I felt this hoof in my ribs and I knew straight away it was bad," Frannie said.

They took him off in the ambulance and by the time I reached the hospital Frannie was coming around from surgery and the doctors were telling Violetta that he would be fine. They had taken out his spleen and then stitched him up again, leaving a big scar on his left side.

"It turns out you don't need a spleen," Umberto said. "Who knew?"

This was the next day, when we all visited Frannie together. Antonia and Leonardo arrived with Umberto and I made room for them on the bed. All four of us squished in around Frannie, eating his hospital food, which he claimed he didn't want, and playing cards on the tray they'd set up in front of him.

"Next time we sit around comparing scars, you will definitely win," Antonia told Frannie, pulling a face at the oozing drains coming out of his belly. He had taken the bandage off to show us how gross it was, even though he wasn't supposed to.

We talked about the race, of course. At the time it had been hard to take it all in, but now we sat and pieced the whole thing together, working on it like it was a giant puzzle, arguing about some parts and laughing at others, and shouting our versions over the top of each other.

"It was very frustrating to watch from the sidelines," Antonia said. "Knowing there was nothing I could do."

"It was just as frustrating to ride in it!" Umberto gave a wry laugh. He was still mortified to have come dead last on Benita. "I rode her as hard as I could, but she simply had nothing to give," he told us.

I told the others how Leonardo had put himself on the line for me, but in his usual fashion he played it down.

"That is what we do for friends." He shrugged it off.

"Yeah, well without you I would've been here in a hospital bed," I said.

"At least then I would've had company," Frannie had piped up.

Even now, it was hard for me to believe I had

escaped the Palio without injury. When I fell from Nico, right there before the finish line, I felt the hooves sweep so close to my head they gave my hair a new parting!

I was still lying in the dirt when the crowd stormed the track and when I saw the hordes of people running towards me, I curled up again, convinced they were coming to beat me, like they'd done to Marco. I braced myself for the kicks and punches. Then I felt the hands clutching at me, and lifting me into the air.

They carried me, flinging me around in mid-air above their heads as they surged beneath me like the sea, singing and weeping and bellowing my name. Not my real name, my Palio name.

Tempesta! Tempesta! Bravest of all Seventeen! Winner of the Palio!

I didn't understand what was going on. I had lost, hadn't I? So why were they cheering for me and crying, tears of joy running down their faces?

"Lola!" The Prior was shouting to me from the crowd below. "Lola! You did it! You won!"

I was bewildered. It was only later when the Prior

and Nonna could explain it properly to me that I understood. I had fallen before I crossed the line. But Nico – my brilliant horse – had finished the race without me. He got across the line a whole length ahead of anyone else and that is how we won the Palio.

That evening, in the great hall of the contrada, the people of the Wolf held a banquet. The Palio banner, which we had won, was now hung in its rightful place above the altar, and Nico stood beneath it as the guest of honour at the head of the table. No one thought it was at all unusual to have a horse at dinner. I sat at the victory table next to Nico and Nonna sat next to me. The Prior and the Capitano sat side-by-side chatting away like best friends. Now that the contrada had won, the Capitano seemed to be well-liked by everyone once more and no one said a word about the fact that he had tried to sell us down the river. I thought that was a little weird, but Nonna just shrugged it off. "The fantino gets the blame when we lose, but the Capitano claims all the glory when we win. That's the way of the Palio."

At the end of the evening everyone wanted to

touch Nico, and he stood so quietly and patiently as they all laid hands on him, as if he knew he was some sort of royalty now. They thought he was enjoying the attention but I could see the tension in him. He wanted it all to be over. He was desperate to be home in the stables of the Castle of the Four Towers with the other horses for company once more.

"Can I take him tonight?" I asked the Prior as the last of the guests began to depart.

The Prior smiled at me. "Of course, Tempesta."

The Prior followed us out into the courtyard where I had first encountered him with scissors in hand, tending his roses. "Daughter of the She-Wolf," he said, "I have something for you to take back to America with you."

He passed me a paper bag.

"Can I open it?"

"Please," the Prior said.

I looked into the bag. "It's full of dirt."

"Yes," the Prior said. "I dug the soil myself from the garden here. One day, Tempesta, you will have children of your own. When you are in labour, put this bag of soil beneath the hospital bed. Then your children will be born above the earth of the Contrada of the Wolf and this will make them true Wolf cubs too, just like you."

"Thank you, Prior."

It was absolutely the weirdest gift I have ever been given.

Nonna took my dirt home to the villa while I rode Nico back to the stables. I had figured he would be exhausted after the race and was surprised to find him full of beans, jogging like a colt as we navigated the steep cobbled streets.

When we reached the driveway of the Castle of the Four Towers and he heard the other horses calling to him, their nickers carrying on the still evening air, he began to give little bucks of excitement. His cry back to them was a shrill clarion call, as if he was announcing his triumphant return. He had left the stables as just another horse, but he was returning as a hero – the winner of the Palio.

When I led him into his stall I saw that Signor Fratelli had already mixed his feed and filled the water trough, and the *spennacchiera*, the pretty head ornament that Nico had worn in the race, had been hung up above his door as a memento.

When I told him goodnight, Nico thrust his muzzle into my arms and snuggled into me. I looked into his soft, deep brown eyes and I saw the light reflected back at me. You couldn't help but see it now, he glowed inside like the fourth of July.

Everything had changed for Nico. He was still a young horse. There would be many more Palios for him. I tried not to think about this as I still couldn't face the idea that there would ever be another rider on his back.

There would be other fantinos for him, just as there would be other horses for me. I was a jockey now. No matter what my dad might say, I was determined that my future, in some way, would be on the track. Nico would not be the only horse I would ride to victory. But he had been the first and he would always be the one I would love best.

Nico wouldn't stop nuzzling me. He seemed to sense that I was upset, he ignored the food in his bucket, clinging to me, and it was his devotion that broke my heart. I didn't want to cry. I hated crying. I brushed the tears roughly from my cheeks, stepped into the courtyard and with shaking hands I bolted the door on his stall and reached out to give him one last stroke on his magnificent muzzle.

"Goodbye, Nico."

I was walking across the stableyard, unable to stop the stupid tears streaming down my face, when I heard the bolt go clunk.

I turned back to see Nico barge the door open with his chest and stroll across the cobbles towards me. He gave this nicker as if to say, "Lola. Not yet, I'm not ready."

I laughed, and raced across the courtyard to him, burying my face in his mane. "You'll always be my horse," I promised him, "and I'll be your girl. But you don't need me now. You're a champion, Nico. I knew it from the first moment we met. And now the world knows it too."

The castle was cloaked in darkness on the lower levels, but there was a light still burning in the southern wing so I went upstairs. The front door to the living room was wide open.

"Hello?"

No reply. I walked around to the southern corridor. "Signor Fratelli?"

"I am here, Lola."

I found him standing there in front of his painting, gazing at it so intently, he didn't even turn his head to acknowledge me.

"I put Nico back in his stall," I said.

"Good, thank you." Signor Fratelli spoke, but his eyes did not waver to meet mine. I didn't know whether I should stay or go.

"I went to the hospital," I added. "I saw Frannie."

"I know," Signor Fratelli said. "I saw him too. Violetta is still there fussing over him, but the boy is going to be fine."

"I was hoping I would see you at the banquet…"

"The Contrada of the Wolf would never welcome me," Signor Fratelli replied.

"What do you mean?" I was shocked. "Of course they would! You trained Nico and he won for them."

"It means nothing. I am still a Porcupine in their eyes. The rivalries in Siena run deep, Lola. Nothing ever changes here."

All this time his eyes had not swayed from the

painting. It looked different at night. The texture and the brushstrokes faded in the soft glow of the lamplight, making the scene become almost real, like an old photograph.

"Violetta told me that painting cost you many of your best Palio horses," I said.

Signor Fratelli nodded. "You have heard of Mariotto and Gianozza?"

"They're like Romeo and Juliet?"

"Yes, they were the original star-crossed lovers. Painted a hundred years before the Englishman wrote his play."

Two lovers, torn apart by their contradas, their love doomed from the start. Just like Signor Fratelli and Nonna. I understood now why the painting meant so much to him, and why he kept his gaze always on Gianozza. The wistful, lovestruck girl on the balcony, with her arm outstretched, imploring him to come to her.

Signor Fratelli raised his handkerchief and wiped his eyes. "If only I had been brave enough to go with her all those years ago." He paused. "I should have tried to find her. Should have told her the truth that I had discovered about Carlo. All those years that she suffered because of me…"

"No," I said softly. "It wasn't your fault. You didn't know where she was. You didn't even know if she was still alive."

Signor Fratelli hung his head. "Do you think she will ever truly forgive me, Lola?"

I took his hand in mine. "I think you know the answer," I said, "but you also know I'm not the one you need to ask."

In case you haven't read *Romeo and Juliet* yet, here's a spoiler alert. They all die and it's a pretty depressing ending if you ask me.

My ending is better. I don't know if you would call it happy, I guess that's up to you.

I had arranged a meeting between Nonna and Signor Fratelli. By then Frannie had come home from the hospital and while me and him and Violetta went together to the stables to feed the horses, Signor Fratelli suggested to my nonna that they continue on into the olive grove beyond and take a tour of the gardens. From the stables we could look down and see the two of them strolling side-by-side, through the sculpted maze of hedges that led down to the orangery.

"It feels like spying," Frannie said.

"Shhh," I told him. "I'm trying to lip read."

I watched as they sat down on a bench under a hazelnut tree. For a long time they talked, and then I saw Nonna reach out and take the signor's hand. He held it in his own, and they spoke some more. Then I saw my nonna say something else and Signor Fratelli looked delighted as he raised her hand, bringing it very gently to his lips to give it a kiss.

When they had finished their walk, we got a taxi home and I asked Nonna what she'd discussed with Signor Fratelli. She went quiet and said, "A great many things." Which made me even more nervous than I was before.

That evening I made us dinner. It was spinach gnocchi, one of the recipes that Nonna had taught me. As I cooked, I fretted over my suspicions as to what the signor might have said.

I put the gnocchi on the table and Nonna took a bite and said, "This is as good as mine, Piccolina!

You've become quite the cook. You don't need me in the kitchen any more."

I felt my stomach lurch. Didn't need her any more? What did that mean?

Nonna took another mouthful and chewed thoughtfully and then in the pregnant silence she said.

"Don't worry, Piccolina. I told him I couldn't marry him."

"What?"

"I know what you are thinking and, yes, he asked me," Nonna said. "But I told him no."

A rush of guilt overwhelmed me. "Nonna!" I said. "No! I'm ruining everything by being selfish that's all! You should stay here, I mean if that's what you want…"

"Oh, Piccolina!" Nonna took my hand and gave it a squeeze. "Sweet child, it isn't because of you that I said no. It's me. I cannot stay here now, any more than I could have back then. Marco knows that deep down, just as I know he cannot leave. But that is OK this time. We both understand each other a little better, I think. I have forgiven him for everything that happened back then. I have forgiven everyone, Piccolina. My parents for keeping me apart from Marco, the contrada for their ridiculous traditions…"

She smiled. "Most important of all, Piccolina, I have forgiven myself. All these years, I truly thought that Carlo had died because of what I had done. I felt so guilty I didn't think I deserved to grieve for him. Now I know the truth, it is like a weight has been lifted from me. Finally I can put the past where it belongs. I can mourn my brother at last."

The next day, Signor Fratelli and Frannie came to our door. It was the last time I would see Frannie for almost five months – he had promised to come and visit us in New York. "It will be Christmas like in the movies," he told me. I didn't have the heart to tell him that those New York movies don't look much like my life in Ozone Park.

Antonia, Umberto and Leonardo were keen to come too. "We can all ride trackwork together with saddles like American jockeys," Frannie said.

"And show off your scars in the bodega," I told

him. I had already phoned home and told my dad about Frannie, and about my own plans to ride trackwork and go to med school at the same time. "There is no way in hell you are riding track, Lola," he'd said. Which was a better response than I expected. Once Nonna got to work on him, I was pretty certain he would agree.

We had packed up the house by the time Frannie and Signor Fratelli arrived. Nonna shut Donatello's visor and gave him a kiss goodbye and she turned the iron key in the lock one last time and put it back beneath the geranium pot. Then the four of us walked together, not in the usual direction towards town, but up into the hills beyond the villa. Here, there was a tiny church and a graveyard right next to it, with ornate headstones, on a hillside overgrown with wildflowers.

I know it sounds strange, but it would be a lovely place to be buried. The view of Siena is beautiful, you can see for miles over oak forests and olive groves and there are loads of my ancestors there. My nonna's mama and papa are both there. We cleaned up their gravestones together, scrubbing the moss from them, even though I thought the moss actually looked quite poetic. On their headstones we put flowers and said a prayer.

Carlo's headstone is right beside theirs. There is the stone with his name and above it stands an angel, very serene and beautiful, with her head bowed and wings outstretched. I gave Nonna some time alone there to talk with her brother. And then when it was my turn, I knelt down and I took the gold medal, the one they presented me with when I won the Palio, and I hung it around the angel's neck.

"It should have been yours," I whispered to Carlo. "You never got the chance to win it again, but I want you to have it."

I like to think about him wearing it up there in heaven, walking through the piazza and charming the girls, being given free olives and cheese by the ladies on the stalls, because he is Carlo Alessi, the greatest fantino in all of Italy, and he has brought glory once more to the Contrada of the Wolf.

RIDING THE WIND:
THE TRUE STORY OF THE PALIO

The ancient Palio was run across the bare brick of the piazza with no dirt track or mattresses along the walls to protect riders or their horses when they crashed and fell.

Four hundred years later there have been a few modernisations, but the rivalry between the seventeen contradas remains as passionate today as it was back then.

The blood feud between Siena's contradas inspired the tale of Mariotto and Gianozza, the star-crossed lovers whose story would eventually become famous as Shakespeare's Romeo and Juliet.

The Palio is not just a horse race. It is considered a matter of life and death and it would take a

riot, an earthquake or a plague to stop it. In 1940 when *Il Duce* declared war against Britain and France, the Palio was prohibited and the race ceased until 1945 when an 'extraordinary' Palio of Peace was held to celebrate Hitler's defeat.

Modern Palio horses are Anglo-Arabs, bred especially for the challenge of the race. They have incredible temperaments and will bond very closely with their fantinos, the jockeys, who must ride them bareback. Whips are allowed in the race but they are used to hit the other riders. Shoving, kicking and punching your opponents is also allowed, earning the Palio its reputation as the world's most dangerous horse race. Throughout the entire history of the Palio, there have been only two female fantinos.

Every girl dreams of becoming a princess.
But this real-life princess has a dream of her own.

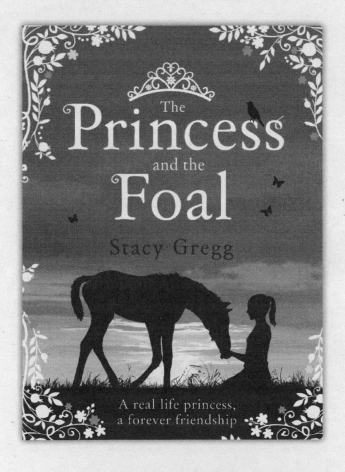

The
Princess
and the
Foal

Stacy Gregg

A real life princess,
a forever friendship

Discover the incredible story
of Princess Haya and her foal.

Two girls divided by time, united by their love
for some very special horses, in this epic
Caribbean adventure.

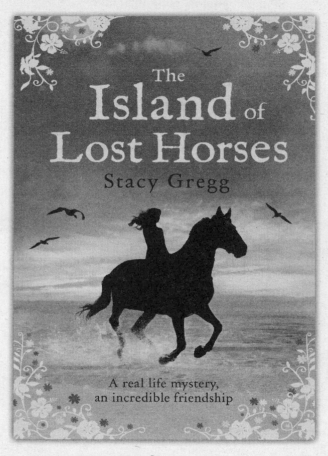

The
Island of
Lost Horses
Stacy Gregg

A real life mystery,
an incredible friendship

Based on the extraordinary true story of the Abaco Barb,
a real life mystery that has remained unsolved
for over five hundred years.

Look out for the next epic story
from Stacy Gregg

The
Diamond
Horse

A Russian palace. A priceless horse.
And a young girl who holds the biggest
secret of all . . .

Coming soon